TINY LITTLE PIECES

JENNIFER LUCIC

Tiny Little Pieces

ISBN: 978-1-7368383-4-1 (paperback)

ISBN: 978-1-7368383-5-8 (hardcover)

ISBN: 978-1-7368383-6-5 (eBook)

Library of Congress Control Number: 2021925362

For Iris Rae.
Lost before we met.
Found in your other half.

CONTENTS

Iris let out a shallow breath and her eyes widened at the little pink plus sign staring back at her. She was twenty-nine years old and had always known it would happen sometime. She had wanted it to happen when things were good. But this was not good. This was her life after the striking text message that brought her world crashing down around her, crushing her dreams, breaking her heart, and proving her mother right.

Her heart raced as the gravity of the situation sunk into her chest. She sucked at the air, her shallow breaths matching the heavy thumping of her heart. Tears streamed from her eyes and bled through her makeup.

"No, no, no... please... this isn't happening," she said, addressing the plastic stick in her hands. The tips of her fingers turned from peach to red to pale as she clenched it. Her pleading turned to groans she uttered through gritted teeth, unsettling into the wailing cries of a woman lost. She was alone now, and that stupid little symbol on a stupid little plastic stick told her she had to think about what it would mean to bring another lonely soul into this world, forced to grow up like she did, without a father.

Unable to look at it anymore, she tossed the drugstore test and watched it crash against the bathroom mirror. Her body fell limp over her bare legs as she collapsed on the toilet and shook in a fury mixed with utter dejection.

"How could he do this to me!" She lifted her head screaming as high and loud as her voice could go. A deep breath replenished her lungs, and she covered her face with her palms in a sob.

The moisture between her legs distracted her. She gathered a wrap of toilet paper in her hand to wipe it off. She stood and inhaled deeply, pulling her panties up. Her body moved through the motions of flushing, and to the sink where she washed her hands—years of conditioning saving her from having to think through the action. A gentle sob escaped her as the soapy water ran between her fingers.

She stared at the weathered condition of her face. Her eyes were puffy and had turned red, and stripes of washed away makeup lined her cheeks. Though she was a beautiful woman with long brown hair, hazel-green eyes, and a thin freckled face, a pretty crier she was not.

"Oh, Jesus, get it together, Iris." She began to fix herself, starting the process with makeup wipes and fresh foundation, and finishing with a few deep composing breaths.

It was Iris' sixteenth birthday. Her emancipated best friend Sarah threw a party for her at the apartment she shared with a co-worker from Bob's Burger Shack. Sarah was a year older, had huge boobs, and a ditzy smile that drove all the boys to her. Iris had learned to live in Sarah's shadow. She was little and shy, with a cup size that never filled more than her tiny hands.

Sarah, on the other hand, had confidence. Iris preferred that Sarah took charge of their social experiences. It was easier for her to take part if she didn't have to talk to people. Sarah would do all the planning, inviting, talking, and all Iris had to do was show up, drink a few beers, and lurk in the glow of Sarah's aura. It was a strategy that worked because there were always others wishing to find a spot in that same space, and like a cat waiting for its mouse, Iris would wait until they came to her. This was how she made friends.

The girls scanned the aisles of their local gas station for their favorite chips and candies, sustenance they'd need for the evening's festivities. They were expecting a full house of kids and grabbed the party size bags and bars as they giggled and gossiped.

"Oh, my god! Did I tell you about the customer I had at work today?" Sarah said. Iris shook her head between glances at the gummy isle. "This dude totally comes in, looks me up and down, and I'm like, hey, and he bends over the counter and writes his number down on a fifty-dollar bill and hands it to me."

"Shut up!" Iris' mouth gaped open.

"No, I'm serious! Tipped me fifty bucks just to give me his number!"

"Oh, my god, that's insane." Iris shook her head as she giggled. "So, are you gonna call him?"

"I already did. He waited for me to get off work, and I gave him a blow job in the parking lot."

"Ahhh!" Iris yelped. "No, you did not! You're such a whore!" The girls laughed at each other as they guffawed about Sarah's *sex-capades*.

Party supplies in hand, Sarah leaned into the plexiglass divider at the register and tugged at her shirt.

"Hey Bob, miss you! How ya' been, babe?" Sarah winked and burst her gum bubble as the clerk's eyes softened and a devilish smile crept onto his face.

"Always good to see you girls." He winked back, rang her up for half of what was in the cart, and threw in a free pack of cigarettes.

"Thanks, babe! You're too sweet to us." Sarah winked again.

"Grab a couple of those twenty-four packs on your way out. Happy birthday, Iris," said Bob, pointing to a stacked display of Bud Light by the door.

"Thanks, Bob!" said Iris, appreciating his birthday gift to her.

"See you next week, hon!" Sarah said as she waved, and she and Iris walked out with their loot.

"So, I have something special for you. Are you ready?" Sarah said as Iris drove away from the station.

"What do you mean?"

"I mean, I have a very special friend coming tonight. For your birthday present!"

"What?" Iris let out a nervous laugh as the anticipation made her grip tighter onto the steering wheel.

"His name is Elijah, an old friend. His brother used to date my sister forever ago. We all used to like, hang out together, they were basically our neighbors, ya' know?"

"Uh, ok..." Iris didn't know what it was like growing up with kids around. She was raised in a house with a quiet cul-de-sac with houses owned by retirees and families with grown-up kids. There were no children in her neighborhood. She spent summers and school breaks in her room, alone with her crafts and bead jewelry. The closest she ever got to making friends was two teenage brothers who lived across the street. They had babysat her once when her mother needed help, but she was never allowed to play with them. *Little girls shouldn't play with teenage boys, it's inappropriate,* her mother always told her.

"Anyway, he's super-hot, and he's about to ship off to the Air Force or something. I told him to come tonight."

"Oh, my god! Like a setup? Like he knows he's supposed to meet me?"

"Yeah."

"Sarah! That's so embarrassing. Why would you?" Iris' face turned red, and her eyes widened to match her gaping mouth.

"What? It's not embarrassing. You're such a cutie, he'll

be totally into you." Sarah scoffed and dismissed the concern with a flip of her wrist and a roll of her eyes.

"No, oh, my god, Sarah. No. This is horrible. I can't believe you did this." Iris shook her head but smiled wide, the laugh behind her voice indicating the opposite of what her words did.

"Iris, I swear, he's super nice and super cute, and he's really into shy girls, so I think you're really gonna like him. Plus, you're only ever this shy when you're sober. And we're gonna fix that."

"I mean, yeah, I guess, but..."

"But nothing! You're sixteen, it's time to dust the cobwebs off. You can't stay a virgin forever. This is happening, so get used to it."

"Wait a minute. Did you tell him I wanted to have sex with him?" Iris' jaw dropped but it wasn't much of a surprise coming from Sarah.

"Well, not in so many words..."

"Ahhhhhh! Sarah!" The small cabin of her VW Beetle filled with the high-pitched yelp of a giddy teenage girl. Sarah laughed and after a few fake moans and protestations, so did Iris, keeping up the laughter the rest of the way back to Sarah's apartment.

THREE

It was already nine p.m. when the girls reached home; their friends were waiting for them outside the door.

"Sup, bitches!" Sarah shouted as she stepped out of Iris' car, leaving the heavy lifting to Iris as she went to greet the party people. Iris pulled two twenty-four packs of Bud Light from the hatchback and locked the car. She tugged on the door latch to make sure it had locked and gave the beeper an extra click, a habit she'd developed after incidents of theft, seeing homeless men taking refuge in the carelessly left open vehicles, and hearing the constant wailing of police sirens that rang through the neighborhood. All served as a reminder to double-click.

"Hey, what's up, Sarah!" Each person had a different way of saying the same words, for one, it became "wassup", for another it was "sup", yet another one said, "waaazzzup".

"Happy birthday, Iris. Here, let me help you with those," one of the boys said, jogging to where she struggled with the packs. Robert was the only person who noticed her, perhaps because she often let him copy off her math homework.

"Oh, thanks. Yeah, there's one around the back, thanks."

Iris pointed to the trunk and carried the other pack into the apartment.

"Okay, mutha fuckers!" Sarah shouted. She flicked on the lights and fiddled with a living room stereo. "Let's get this party started!"

A cacophony of voices agreeing with Sarah erupted inside.

"Yeah!"

"Go, Sarah!"

"Woo-hoo!"

"Where's the beer?" someone said, just as Iris walked in with it. With complete focus on her task, she tried to avoid the unexpected attention as everyone looked at her. She headed for the kitchen with her head down, Robert close behind.

"Right here!" Sarah intervened. Iris and Robert placed the packs of beer on a cheap folding dining table that swayed with the weight of the packages. The sound of the top 40 radio station Sarah had tuned into played in the background as everyone grabbed a can and popped the tab.

"Ahhhhh. Now that's a good beer!" Robert said, chugging it down and crushing the can in his hands.

Iris laughed and rolled her eyes.

"Whoo!" he shouted and grabbed another beer.

Iris popped open a can for herself, took a sip, and cringed at the warm bubbly taste. She stacked the rest of the cans in the empty fridge. When she finished stocking the fridge, she stood in the corner and surveyed the room for fresh faces, taking slow sips. More people showed up, but all of them she had seen before. There was no sign of the mystery man Sarah had roped in for her, and although she had shown a complete lack of interest in the setup, she couldn't help but keep an eye out for him.

BY TEN-THIRTY, there was still no sign of her birthday present. Iris had downed several beers and was feeling a lot more relaxed than when the night began. She allowed herself to mingle, becoming part of conversations about other parties the kids were going to or how boring Ms. Flannery's class was that week.

"Iris! Iris!" Sarah called out. She turned around to find her standing at the doorway. "I have someone I want you to meet!" Iris looked at the tall person standing next to Sarah. His sharp features were accentuated by light mocha skin. Her eyes followed his arms covered in tattoos that slinked up his neck. An unexpected jolt of electricity struck her when she noticed the snake bite piercings on his lips.

"Hi," he said s in a deep, all-consuming voice, the baritone sending shivers into her, rousing the butterflies in her belly. "I'm Elijah. I hear it's your birthday?"

"Uh, hi... yeah, thanks." Iris' face flushed red as she extracted her gaze from him.

"I brought you a present," he said holding up a handle of Jack Daniels.

"Oh, wow. For me?" Iris got excited at the sight of the alcohol, distracting herself from the initial surprise of the attractive boy.

"For you! Take a shot with me?"

"Yeah, okay."

"Yes." Sarah chimed in. "Shots!"

A few others followed them to the flimsy kitchenette and took shot after shot until the handle was half empty and Iris was energetically fuzzy. As the party of thirsty teenagers clamored for the alcohol, Elijah poured each glass with a smile and an offer for more. He and his gift had brought the party alive as more people flocked to him. Either for a free shot or to bask in his presence, Iris couldn't tell.

Several shots in, Sarah had given up, raising her hands in defeat. She couldn't drink anymore and sashayed to the makeshift dance floor in the living room. Iris called her a pussy and gulped at least one more, Elijah laughing next to her.

"You wanna dance?" Elijah asked Iris with a cocked head and exaggerated smile.

"Dance? Oh, I'm not... uh... I can't dance." Despite the copious amount of alcohol swirling through her tiny body, she couldn't escape her tendency to shy away, avert her eyes, and deny his obvious advances. Elijah held out his hand to her.

"Wow, you have really nice hands!" She said as she noticed his pristine, manicured skin and nails.

Elijah chuckled. "Gotta take care of those fingernails. Nothing worse than a dirty fingernail." He took her hand. "Come on. This is my favorite song." Elijah grabbed her hand and led her to the crowded dance floor, choosing the center.

"This is your favorite song, too? B. Spears?"

"Hell yeah! This is my jam!" He playfully swayed his hips and grinded into her like a male stripper.

She laughed. "You're an amazing dancer."

The melody swept into lyrics, and he sang along. Cute banter turned to a heated expression as he pulled her hips into his and forced their bodies to move together. As he mouthed the lyrics, he brought his lips within inches from hers, maintaining eye contact, further closing the gap. She tried to look away, their faces too close for comfort, but he lifted her chin and gave her a deep seductive gaze.

Her heartbeat thumped aching to jump out of her chest. The music grew louder in her head, melting away the raucous laughter and drowning out the voices of the rest of the party. It was like Elijah and she were the only ones there.

Iris' breath turned heavy as she closed her eyes and anticipated his next move. She was ready for her first kiss. Electricity powered through her veins, and she leaned in.

"Oh, my god, I love this song! Unusual... so unusual..." Sarah's drunken rendition broke through the intimacy, butchering their little bubble. Iris snapped back into the living room full of drunk, dancing high school kids.

"Yeah, it's a good one. Elijah likes it too." Iris broke away from Elijah's hold as Sarah bumped into them.

"So! Are you guys having fun?" Sarah asked, swaying the entire time.

"I'm so drunk," Iris said, forcing a laugh and turning her face away as she felt it flush.

"Yay, happy birthday. I love you."

"I love you too."

"You wanna go smoke a cigarette?" Sarah asked. "Elijah, you wanna come?"

"No, no, I don't smoke. You guys go ahead, I'll be right here." The moment gone, Iris nodded and walked with Sarah to the sliding glass door leading out to the patio.

FOUR

The air around the patio was stiff and murky, the space filled with kids smoking. Iris and Sarah had picked up the vice freshman year when Sarah discovered where her parents hid their cigarettes, packs and packs stacked on top of each other in the freezer. Sarah would wait for an opportunity to smuggle some and sold them for two dollars a pack at school. Her parents never noticed when one or two went missing. It became too easy to start smoking. Sarah gave her a discount—one dollar a pack—homie hook-up price she called it.

"So? How's it going?" Sarah asked, a cigarette between her lips waiting to be lit.

"Oh, my god. He's so cute," Iris replied. "I think he likes me. I didn't even want to dance, but he was like, 'oh yeah, you gotta'. And then, while we were on the floor, he started singing the coolest song of the year to me. And I think we were about to kiss. He's like, my dream come true!" Iris grabbed the lighter from Sarah and lit her cigarette.

"Yay. That's so cool. I hope you guys go get freaky."

Sarah laughed but Iris recoiled hearing Sarah say it out loud.

" No..." Iris shook her head. "Wait... You think he wants to?"

"Oh, I know he wants to. No guy sings B. Spears to a girl he doesn't wanna bone." Both girls erupted in a fit of giggles.

As Iris inhaled the smoke, she looked toward the dark parking lot, the only view from the patio. The cars swayed like they were underwater. Her face contorted into puzzlement until a wave of nausea overtook her, and her world turned upside down and around in circles.

"Ugh, I don't feel so good," she said, holding her stomach, bent over at the waist.

"Oh, no. Are you okay? What's wrong?" Concerned, Sarah crouched and rubbed Iris' back.

"I don't know, I think..." Iris couldn't finish her sentence before vomit projected out of her mouth and into the bushes.

"Oh, no. Honey." Sarah continued to rub her back with one hand and gathered her hair with the other. "It's okay. Get it all out. You're fine. Get it all out." Her voice had taken on an almost nursery rhyme melody. Iris found it calming.

Iris finished puking and allowed Sarah to guide her back inside, one arm around her neck and shoulders, still hunched over, no longer able to stand upright on her own.

"Elijah, can you help me?" Sarah called out as the girls reentered the apartment.

"Oh shit, yeah." Elijah came to gather Iris by her other arm, but his height made it difficult for him to stabilize her. "Hold on," he said as he released her from Sarah's hold and picked her up, and cradled her in his arms. Iris, still lucid but unable to react to the moment, smiled with her eyes closed and draped her arms around his neck. "Where to?" Elijah asked.

"This way, come on." Sarah took the lead, and Elijah followed her down a small hallway to her bedroom. "Here. Put her on the bed." Elijah complied and rested Iris on Sarah's bed. It was a bed Iris had been drunk in several times before and recognized its fuzzy zebra striped comforter and thin pillows.

"Thank you. I love you. Sorry, I puked in your bushes," Iris mumbled.

"It's okay, honey. You just relax. It's your birthday."

"Yeah, happy birthday, Iris. Nice meeting you." Elijah chuckled and said his goodbyes.

"Bye. I love you, too." The last word Iris drunkenly fumbled through before she fell asleep.

IRIS' eyes fluttered open to the sound of slapping skin. It was dark, but moonlight peeked through the window and illuminated enough of the room for Iris to make out the source. On the floor, a few feet away, a pair of large bare breasts jiggled in the dim light, and the silhouette of Sarah's face was hidden in darkness. Iris chuckled to herself and covered her mouth so as not to make a sound. Sarah's naked thighs straddled another body between them. Iris adjusted her head to identify the face. Metal snake bite piercings glittered in soft shadow, next to the same thick lips that had almost been hers earlier that night. A tattooed male chest pulsated in rhythm with Sarah's body on top.

A sting crawled into Iris' chest and tightened her throat, her chuckle gone. A guttural moan in deep baritone confirmed it was Elijah. She resisted the temptation to make her intrusion known and kept herself frozen on the bed. It would be over soon, she reasoned, and tried to put herself back to sleep. She closed her eyes and clenched them tighter with each moan. Every smack of skin against skin made her muscles tense until she was a knotted rubber ball.

"We can never tell Iris about this," Sarah whispered as she bounced on top of him.

"Why?" Elijah asked, suppressing a grunt.

"Because! I brought you here for her and this is fucked up."

"No, it's not. She passed out. I was down for her, but..."

"I know, but like..." Sarah stopped her thrusts. "Look, she's my best friend, and I love her, but I know this would crush her. She has some weird thing about rejection. Her dad abandoned her when she was a baby, and like, she can't be alone or whatever. She told me how much she likes you and this would just be a total slap in the face. I can't do that to her."

"Okay, that's a lot of information, but whatever, just keep going." The conversation ended and Sarah resumed the task requested of her. Silent tears dripped out of Iris' eyes as she sunk into total defeat.

FIVE

AUGUST 12, 2016

"I'm quitting my job," Iris told Sarah during their weekly Marg MeetUp at the local taco shop; it was the halfway point between their workplaces and on the way to their shared apartment. Iris worked at a gallery in the Haight & Ashbury district, and Sarah worked as a family therapist downtown. Iris was lucky enough to find something in the art industry, putting her degree in modern art to good use.

"What? Again? Why? Don't tell me this is because of Jason."

Iris shrugged and looked down at her strawberry margarita, swirling the ice cubes around with her straw. Jason was the gallery owner and the man who had hired her. Admittedly, she believed she only got the job because Jason was interested in her. He'd never made it obvious, but he didn't have to. Iris understood what men were thinking when they looked at her with their wide eyes and excited smiles. By her second week at the gallery, Jason asked her to get drinks. He was nice, she was single, and she accepted the invitation.

The problem was that there wasn't anything interesting about him. He was an average-looking guy with greasy hair and a nose that looked like it was always turned up, but maybe that was his personality. The date continued through drinks and back to his apartment, where he politely offered her a nightcap but she cut right to the chase. They had unimaginative and pleasureless sex. He, on top of her, and she, after giving it a good few minutes to impress, wondering if she would make it home in time for the late show.

There were a few more dates, and a few more nights of the same sad sex. Iris kept wanting to believe he would get better, that she liked him, and this wasn't a pattern. She would grow tired of the interactions and tell herself she was ready to move on. It was a cycle that had repeated itself since the first guy she'd met and dated in college to poor Jason, who never had a chance.

"Iris, you cannot keep quitting every job you have because you get tired of the men you fuck there."

"It's not that... not *just* that."

"Then what? What else is it?"

"He's just being super clingy, and the sex is super lame. I just can't. I don't know. He's weird."

"He's weird? Because you don't like the sex? Have you tried using your voice to tell him what you like and how you want it? Be vocal! Tell him what you need from him. What are you so afraid of?"

"Nothing. Nothing, shh." Iris tensed, her shoulders hunched, and dropped her voice down to a whisper. "It's nothing, I just, I can't do that with someone. That feels super... intimate."

"Oh please, Iris. You're twenty-four years old. You're not a virgin. You can tell a guy what you want him to do to you. Are you afraid you'll like it and then it'll be harder to leave or something? Ya know, because of-"

"It's because of nothing, Sarah. It's just- I don't-"

Sarah held up her hands to stop Iris from burying herself in the lies she'd told herself her whole life. "Look, I've known you forever. I know what your issues are. If you don't like Jason, that's fine. But running away from every promising relationship isn't helping you get over them. You need a real boyfriend. You've been using our relationship to substitute a romantic one and you need more than that."

"Okay, whatever, Sarah. I don't wanna talk about this anymore." Iris shook her head and took a long sip of her drink. "Anyway, I have an interview tomorrow at that glass studio, Artful Glass, down the street," she said, changing the subject and adding a cheerful note into her voice. "They're looking for a curator and it's cool because it's closer to your office, so we can like carpool and stuff."

"Cool, Iris. That's great. I hope you get it." Sarah let out a sigh.

SIX

AUGUST 13, 2016

Iris arrived at the glass studio fifteen minutes ahead of her nine-a.m. interview. She waited patiently in the lobby and admired the artful pieces of colorful blown glass that adorned the shelves and counter spaces.

"Iris?" a voice called out from behind the reception counter.

"Yes, hi. I'm Iris," she said as she stood to greet the older woman waiting for her. The woman was striking in her worn overalls and old t-shirt, and long silver hair braided down each side of her head. She looked like a classic hippie type; the kind Iris found enchanting. Growing up, she must have watched countless YouTube videos of them dancing like maniacs at Woodstock and wishing she had been a part of their heyday.

"Hello, Iris. I'm Marie. My son owns this studio. I'm a local artist here. He and I will interview you today." Marie held out her hand in a greeting.

"Hi, Marie. Nice to meet you. Beautiful studio you have here."

"Oh, thank you. Please follow me." Marie led Iris

through the office and spoke about the different areas as they passed. There was a reception, a small space for the sales team and the administrative team. The office space was tiny compared to the studio in the back where the artists blew glass and cured their pieces. Occasionally, they held open classes anyone could sign up for to learn from the glassblowers and try it out for themselves. Iris offered polite nods as she listened before being shown the door to a small conference room. "Right in here."

A man sat waiting at the table. He had light mocha skin, tattoos running up and down his arms, and...

"Iris?"

"Oh, my god. Elijah?" Iris' voice and wide eyes betrayed a giddy excitement as she tried to hide her surprise.

"Wow, Iris! It's been years. Get in here." Professionalism left the room as the two casually embraced like old friends.

She remembered him well. Her first crush and the boy from whom she had wanted her first kiss. The night of her birthday lived in her mind in infamy, circling through all the what-ifs her mind could carry.

In the immediate weeks following that night, her phone rang occasionally, his name lit up the caller ID. A smile crept onto her face each time, but she never answered. Answering would have meant confronting the moonlit vision of him and Sarah, what they'd done right under her nose, and that was something she'd never been prepared to do. It was easy to stay friends with Sarah and pretend she never saw what she saw. She resolved that it was better this way, that she could remain best friends with Sarah and never have to truly be alone. Pushing it down and inside herself kept her life steady and her friendship with her only friend intact. Elijah would stop calling soon enough, and he did.

Over the next eight years, she thought about him often and silently. About how things might have been different had she not gotten so drunk and sick. Maybe it would have been her on top of him instead of Sarah? Maybe they would have never lost touch? Maybe he would still be in her life? Either way, she was here now, standing before him, dumbfounded at the kismet of it all. At that moment, life made sense. It was the gift of a second chance. It was fate.

"Oh, looks like you two already know each other," Marie said.

"Oh, yeah," Elijah said, clearing his throat. "Mom, this is my old friend, Iris. We met briefly right before I joined the Air Force. What's it been, like, eight years?" He looked at Iris, who smiled and nodded in agreement.

"All right," Marie said, breaking the silence as Elijah and Iris stared at each other with toothy smiles. "Well, should we have an interview, or should I just let you two get reacquainted?"

"I got it, Mom. Thanks." Elijah didn't take his eyes off Iris as he addressed his mom.

"Call me if you need anything." Marie walked out of the room.

"My god, it's good to see you!" Elijah said. Iris felt her legs tingle.

"I can't believe you remember me. It's been so long," she said, her high-pitched excitement in complete contrast to his sultry drawl.

"Of course, I remember you... Hey, by the way. I..." Elijah paused before finishing the sentence and his face became unsure.

"It's fine. I couldn't expect you to keep calling forever. It's really nice to see you, though."

Elijah reached out to touch Iris' shoulder and offered a warm smile. "Shall we?" He extended his arm and gestured her to a chair. Iris smiled and sat. He followed and sat down right beside her.

The interview began, and between questions about her education and work history, Elijah asked her about her love life and when he could take her out for drinks. Iris tried her best to answer the serious questions but blushed through the personal ones. By the time they finished, Iris' face had developed a permanent beet-red hue and her never-ending smile kept the inside of her lips plastered to her teeth.

"Okay, okay. I'm done playing with you. Sorry, I couldn't resist; you're just too cute," Elijah said.

Iris blushed again and directed her gaze to the floor so he couldn't see her wide grin.

"Look, the job is yours, of course. Will you let me take you out tonight to celebrate? You just landed the job at the hottest new studio in town, pretty big deal."

"Um, okay..." She hid her throbbing heart and the inward scream of euphoric pleasure at being asked out by her first crush.

"Great. Meet me back here at eight. I know a cool little spot, and later I can show you around the studio a bit."

"Sounds good."

"Oh, and you start Monday." Elijah gave her a brief hug.

Iris walked herself out of the room and the office, each step metaphorically lifting her off the ground until her feet were floating inches above the corporate-style carpeting. Her heart fluttered as the butterflies erupted in the pit of her stomach.

SEVEN

She couldn't even wait to cross the threshold before bringing the phone to her ear. Iris had already thumbed through her contacts, found Sarah's name, and clicked the green call icon.

"Hey, what's up?" Sarah answered, her voice hurried.

"You will not believe who I just ran into." The enthusiasm in Iris' voice made up for the lack in Sarah's.

"Um, hold on, I got it... John Lennon? No, Tupac!"

"Ugh." Iris rolled her eyes. "Oh, my god, you're so dumb. No, Elijah! Elijah!" She repeated the name, still having trouble with the reality of it herself. "He's my new boss."

"Shut. Up."

"No, I swear. He owns Artful Glass, the studio. He wants to take me out to dinner."

"Wow! Are you gonna go?"

"Um, yes. Of course I'm going. He just wants to show me around the studio a bit and introduce me to his business, I guess."

"I bet he does. Sarah's voice dropped as she twisted into an innuendo.

"Shut up. It's not like that. He's, my boss. We're just gonna be friends," she said as if speaking the words would make it true, even though she knew better.

"Oh, sure, sure. Whatever you say. Well, you crazy kids have fun. I have to get back to work, but call me after and let me know how it went."

"Okay, bye." Iris hung up. She hopped and skipped and happy-danced the rest of the way to her car.

IRIS SHUFFLED through her closet for the perfect outfit. Something sexy without appearing desperate. She didn't want to give off the wrong impression, but she also couldn't help but be excited at the possibilities of what the night might bring.

She settled on an army green pencil skirt that hugged her figure and a tan ribbed bodysuit. In high school, she'd carried her thin frame with flat curves. But estrogen had been good to her over the years, gifting her with flared hips and a body that could have mused poets. She straightened her hair and darkened the makeup around her eyes and on her lips. A pair of tan suede wedge heels completed the look.

Iris arrived at the studio and pulled into the parking lot. She gripped the wheel tighter as she felt her hands shake from nerves. With sheer will and determination, she coerced her hands to steady. When they didn't, she shook them into compliance. Elijah was already waiting outside for her.

"You made it," he said as she opened her door.

"Yup, here I am." Iris smiled like nothing was wrong, but inside her heartbeat careered in her chest and blood rushed into the tips of her ears and lips, making them hot.

"Perfect." He smiled and bent down in a polite greeting reaching out his arm. She laced it into hers and let him help her out of the car.

At the restaurant, they talked like friends and bantered like prospective lovers, the tension between them rising. A pressure that had been building for eight years, growing from an idea of intimacy, manifested into a tingling warmth that traveled from her chest down to her thighs and concentrated between them.

The heat confused her. It wasn't like her to get physically hot for a man. But as she watched his lips move, she understood it to be a craving. She wanted him and thought about what that might mean. Her mind dripped with desire as she imagined how it would feel to be locked under his body. His voice drifted off into the distance, and she let herself revel in her fantasy. Her eyelids sank to half-closed and the corners of her lips tucked up.

She snapped back into reality when she realized she was staring. Scared her face was giving her away like a window into her private thoughts, she shook herself out of it. Metaphorically dousing her head with the glass of water sitting only an arms-length away from her, she imagined the sensation of icy water cooling the warmth that was emanating from her thighs. She found herself in the middle of a conversation she had no memory of. He was talking about price sheets but she had no recollection of the context. Changing the subject was the only thing she could do to save herself.

"So, it doesn't feel like it, but I'm realizing that I don't know anything about you, or your life, or anything," Iris said.

Elijah nodded at her and took a sip of his wine. "Okay, I'll give you the cliff notes. I grew up here, Downtown... there are five of us total. All boys. I have a brother who lives in Texas and three half-brothers. My beautiful mother, whom you've already met, has been through a lot."

"You mean because she raised five kids?"

"No, not because of that. The truth is my mom struggles with a pretty intense pill addiction. She got into some bad stuff when she was younger and met my dad in Tent City. Go figure, he turned out to be a piece of shit. But she's doing better. The studio has been a great outlet for her, for both of us."

"Oh... It's so nice that you two can share that."

"Yeah, we have a good time. Plus, I can keep an eye on her." Elijah laughed. Iris joined him for the sake of being polite.

"And how did you get into glass blowing?"

"A guy I met in the Air Force told me about it. He talked about it like it was the most interesting thing in the world. So, I tried it, and I was hooked. The focus, the patience, discipline. The anxiety that at any moment, if you stop respecting the glass, it *will* shatter itself just to let you know. Crash! The sound of broken glass is one hell of a wake-up call. Having that kind of control, without really being in control is powerful."

Iris watched him describe his passion in awe. "I agree. I love the pieces you have in your studio."

"Speaking of, why don't you let me show you? You wanna get outta here?"

Iris nodded and took his hand.

EIGHT

"Okay," Elijah said as he flicked on the lights that lined the ceiling. The space came awake with the flush of brightness and the resounding clicking as each sconce burned. "This is where the magic happens." He stretched out his arms and presented the open area to her. As they walked, he pointed out the various tools and contraptions. He turned on furnaces and machines, and the whirring brought the empty building to life. While they waited for the heat to build in the furnace, he explained how they melt the glass, shape the glass, and cool the glass. The words left his lips with excitement and his lust for the art became palpable in the air.

"Come here," he whispered and lightly tugged on her hand to bring her closer to the orange glow of the glass furnace. He guided her through the steps and showed her how to gather the molten glass onto the blowpipe, and roll it onto the marver. He stood behind her, his body close as he showed her how to dip the glass into broken pieces of colored shards and said, "This gives it color."

She was like putty in his hands, her body a mannequin

to his demands. Each controlled movement sent an electric buzz from her brain down into her erogenous zones.

"Now, do it like this..." A whisper in her ear, his cheek against hers. As they twisted the blowpipe, a wave crashed through her that nearly knocked her off her feet.

"Whoa!"

He smiled, steadying her. She lowered her gaze to the ground, an embarrassed grin spreading across her face.

"You ok there, Demi?"

She was puzzled until she got the reference, and let out a chuckle. "Oh, does that make you Patrick Swayze then? You complimenting me or yourself?" They laughed together.

Iris swayed. "Um, sorry, I think I'm getting a little woozy from the fire... and the wine." It wasn't wooziness, it was an overabundance of endorphins that rushed through her synapses in ways she was not prepared for or even knew was possible.

"Here, come here. Sit down." He pulled her away from the furnace and sat down on the concrete floor covered only by an old Persian rug, littered with burn marks, and motioned for her to follow. The chemical cocktail coursing through her body pulled her to listen. "Relax, you seem tense."

A classic line she'd heard before and knew what came next—an uncomfortable back rub, the aggressive petting, and thirsty lips. But this was different. The thought of his lips meeting hers didn't frighten her, it warmed her.

The back rub did come, but it wasn't uncomfortable. His hands gripped her shoulders and slid down her back in a slow and relaxing motion, melting her spine into his hands like the glass on the blow stick. His eyes were focused on hers; she could see a fire burning in them as they reflected off the glow of the furnace.

"Can I kiss you?" It was the first time anyone had ever asked.

"Yes."

His lips were soft, and they tangled into hers. She felt her heart burst in a firework of euphoria that traveled through the rest of her body. His hands caressed her in tune with the pressure of his mouth on hers. She let out a soft moan that surprised even her.

"Is this okay?" He pulled away to ask, smiling and nuzzling his nose on her face.

She couldn't speak, but nodded and put her lips back on his. The passion burned between their bodies brighter than the fire behind them. They ripped away their clothing and crashed into each other. Connected in a lover's embrace, she took him in and gasped at the slow pain.

"Are you okay?"

"Yes, keep going, please!" Her voice struck a high note as she begged him not to stop. With her eyes closed, she let herself feel everything he gave her.

"COME HERE," Elijah said. Their bodies buzzed as they lay next to each other, beads of sweat clinging to their skin. "The floor's hard, don't hurt your head. Here, lay on my chest." His sturdy arm swallowed her up in a half-embrace.

"Well, that was fun," he said, as she squeezed her body closer to his.

"Yeah, I guess that's one way to get to know your boss." They both laughed.

"Oh, you do this with all your bosses?"

"No, no! Actually... Not like this, not like, as much as I wanted this to be this." Iris offered a nervous giggle. Not even she knew what she was saying anymore.

"Oh?" Elijah held out the word in an exaggerated joke. "So, you admit you wanted me?"

"Shut up!" She playfully slapped his bare chest making him chuckle.

"Wait, did you just take advantage of me?" Elijah asked as he shot his head up and he looked at her with a shit-eating grin on his face.

"Oh, my god," Iris covered her eyes and giggled.

"Damn, I feel so violated!" he said, continuing with the charade.

A few more minutes of cuddling and neither of them could stand the rug-covered concrete any longer. Elijah pulled Iris to her feet and helped her gather her clothes before grabbing his own. It was late, and the excitement-filled night had exhausted her.

"So... see you Monday?" Elijah said as he walked her to her car and opened the door for her.

"Yeah, see you Monday." Iris smiled at him and sat down in the driver's seat. Before she closed the door, he leaned in and kissed her.

"Bye," he said as he stepped back and waited for her to drive away.

NINE

AUGUST 15, 2016

Iris showed up to work that following Monday, not entirely sure of herself. She questioned whether her rendezvous with Elijah was a drunken mistake and if she was stupid for showing up and expecting a job from a man she'd already slept with. She wondered if she'd let silly teenage-girl fantasies cloud her better judgment. Her gaze fixed on the entrance, she wondered if it was too late to get her job back at the art gallery with Jason and cringed at the thought.

She took a deep breath, gathered her strength, and got out of the car. Before she could make her way in, the door swung open, revealing Elijah on the other side. The sight of him standing there smiling melted her doubt. To bask in his aura was the only place she wanted to be.

"Good morning!" he greeted. "Come on. I want you to meet everyone." Elijah reached for her hand and pulled her inside. His energy was infectious, and she pepped up instantly, his smile like an IV dripping caffeine straight to her veins.

He introduced her to the staff and showed her the ins and outs of the place. The two of them moved in sync, almost skipping like school children at morning recess, offering hellos and shaking hands with everyone that crossed their path. Iris met the assistant, the other artists, and Marie, whose warm smile and hug made her feel welcome.

"And this is your office," said Elijah, the last stop on the official tour.

"This is great, thank you, uh..." Iris paused and looked at Elijah with a puzzled face. "What do you want me to call you?" she asked, half wondering where to draw the line between professionalism and love-making-on-concrete.

"You can call me whatever you want... as long as it starts with honey, baby, sexy face, or love of my life!" Elijah looked at her with a straight face, but Iris couldn't control herself. She burst into laughter.

"You did not just tell me to call you Sexy Face!" Iris snorted.

"Uh, I think I did, and Sexy Face wants you to meet him for lunch in the back. Noon. Good?"

"Uh-huh. Sure thing..."

Elijah looked at her with wide expectant eyes.

Iris rolled her own eyes and whispered the words, "Sexy Face."

"Alright, see you for lunch. Have a great morning!" Elijah slapped the door frame as he showed himself out, shouting as he went. "Sexy Face!"

FIVE MINUTES BEFORE NOON, Iris peered into her compact mirror and did a quick touch-up. She stood to straighten her clothing and took a last look at herself when Elijah knocked, startling a yelp out of her.

"It's just me, S.F. Ready for lunch?"

Iris laughed, nodded, and followed him out.

THEY ARRIVED at the Tap House. A friendly hostess greeted him by name and offered to take them to "his" table.

"Alright, here we are. Simon will be your server today, and don't worry, Elijah, I already have your whiskey neat on the way," said the hostess as she laid their menus in front of them and walked away.

"Thank you!"

"Whiskey neat?" Iris cocked her head to the side like a puppy trying to understand.

"Yeah, they know me here. This is the client-schmoozing spot. People love to buy expensive art when they're drunk. So, how do you like the studio so far?" Elijah changed the subject faster than his drink order came to the table.

IRIS SAT through her Caesar salad while Elijah sipped on his drink, and then another. They exchanged small talk, but mostly it was a quiet lunch. Elijah's attention stayed focused on the basketball game highlights playing on all the TVs that outlined the bar area. He'd missed it and wanted a chance to catch what he called the cliff notes.

His tone didn't change, not anytime through the three whiskeys. He remained level-headed and appeared sober. By the end of lunch, Iris felt confident enough to question him. "Three lunch drinks, hmmm?" She chuckled, wanting to keep things playful.

"What can I say, my mom always told me, if you're gonna do something, do it right."

Iris' eyes shot open as she stumbled into her old childhood home. She looked around trying to gain her bearings and noticed vintage yellow wallpaper, oddly reminiscent.

A little girl stood in front of a man Iris recognized as her father, jumping and shouting "daddy" and dancing around in circles. The man remained stone-faced and empty-eyed staring at the television screen. Iris watched the pathetic display of her younger self begging for her father's attention. *Pitiful*, the older Iris thought.

"Stop it!" Iris said to her younger self. She crossed her arms over her chest and gritted her teeth when she heard no response.

Young Iris, in a last attempt to win her father's affection, somersaulted in front of him and yelled, "Daddy, look at me!" But her attempt was thwarted by a side table as her tumbling body bumped into it, sending a glass vase crashing to the ground. Tiny little pieces of glass scattered on the floor.

Her father, eyes still glued to the television, gave a half-smirk. "If you're gonna do something, do it right!"

"Hey!" Elijah's voice broke through the nightmare. Iris opened her eyes and was back in the bar, sitting calmly while Elijah signed for the check.

Elijah took the last sip from his glass and replaced his credit card in his wallet. "You ready?"

TEN

The way back to the gallery was spent in quiet reflection.

"Thanks for joining me for lunch. I'll see you at quitting' time," Elijah said and went into the studio, where he stayed for the rest of the day.

The whole experience left Iris feeling strange. She hated remembering her father and that god-damned yellow wallpaper. Her father had been an alcoholic and she knew what it was to watch a grown man drink enough to inebriate a horse but not show it. Three whiskeys and the only thing that changed for Elijah was his breath. Was he an alcoholic? Or was he just accustomed to entertaining clients and really needed that afternoon pick-me-up? Did it matter? Iris cycled through excuses, so she didn't have to think about the consequences of what it meant to be attracted to a man like her father.

She shook her head and put the thought out of her mind. It wasn't her business to worry about Elijah's drinking habits and she still needed to familiarize herself with the office, daily tasks, and sort out the mess left behind by the last curator.

By the time the five o'clock bell rang, Iris had disappeared into her computer screen. Her assistant, Jessica, a young college girl working for college credit, popped in to say goodbye.

Iris looked up at her, confused at the ringing.

"That's the bell. Yes, we have an actual bell here." Jessica laughed and adjusted the glasses on her face, pushing them up her nose.

"Oh. It's five already? The day went by so fast. Thanks for all your help today, Jessica. See you tomorrow."

Jessica waved and followed the rest of the staff out the front entrance. The back door to the studio swung open. The group of artists led by Elijah walked in one by one.

"Happy hour! Happy hour!" Elijah cupped his hands around his mouth, cheering and shouting. "Tavern! Happy hour!"

"Hey, so after work, a group of us get together at The Tavern. You coming?" He said as he leaned against the door frame, crossing one foot over the other.

"Oh, um..." She took a moment to think about it, the same uneasy feeling she'd got after lunch making a reappearance. "I actually have plans tonight."

"Oh, I see how it is. Ditching me already, huh?" It was like everything that came out of his mouth was a joke, and charming at that. Her heart thumped and she laughed.

"No, no. Nothing like that. My mom. She wants to get together to talk about my first day. You know how moms are..."

"Do I?" He smiled at her but his eyes were stone cold.

"Oh, uh... I just meant..." Iris felt a lump in her throat, embarrassed at the faux pas.

"I'm joking. Joking. Tell Ma I said hi and next time invites me too." He winked again, waved, and walked away.

His confidence was overzealous, enough to diffuse the self-reprimand.

"HI, SWEETHEART." Iris's mother, June, answered the front door and pulled her daughter in for a giant hug. "Honey. I'm so glad you're here. How was your first day?" The questions had begun before Iris even stepped through the threshold.

"Hi, Mom. It was good. Good. I have lots to tell you."

"Wonderful. Well, come in, I made your favorite dessert!"

The women gabbed like girlfriends. June was special to Iris. They were all the other had after a dramatic exit by Iris' father when Iris was seven. The details remained fuzzy, but Iris remembered a childhood full of anger, screaming and fear. Her father would come home late, drunk, making enough noise to wake Iris and send her to her favorite spot under the bed. She became so accustomed to that spot that she furnished it with a blanket and pillow and her favorite dolly. As her mother screamed, and her father yelled, Iris remained huddled and hidden until she fell asleep, only to be woken again by the thud of her mother being pushed, hit, or knocked down.

Some nights the fights lasted longer. Sometimes she would listen to her mother wail about other women, calling them whores. Other times her mother would concede to avoid a harder hit. On the nights the fighting seemed to go on forever, Iris would wake up to sunlight peering through the window and onto the hardwood floor, the darkness under the bed undisturbed. She would watch her mother's feet come into the room, and bend down until her mother's beaten and exhausted face met her gaze. With hardly any strength left, her mother would pull her from her hiding spot to begin the day.

Despite the sound of breaking glass and furniture being thrown around, and the bumps and bruises on her mother the next morning, she loved her father. The attention she craved from him, made her desire his affection even more because it wasn't given to her.

After he left, the quiet made it almost difficult to sleep. Iris spent what felt like forever tossing and turning, waiting for the night to force her brain to shut down until the sun arose. In the months and years after his departure, Iris clung to her mother, never understanding why she felt scared in the quiet silence, why the sound of nothing made her heartbeat into her ears.

"There's something else, Mom." Iris was ready to tell June about Elijah.

"What's that, honey?"

"So, my new boss. His name is Elijah. I don't know if you remember, but in high school, I had this intense crush on a boy named Elijah."

"Oh, of course, I remember. You met him at a birthday party. Whatever happened to him?"

"Yes. Anyway, he's my boss now."

"No!" June gasped.

"I know. It's crazy. Like, fate? Hello?" Iris laughed a little while her mother listened in disbelief. Iris told her mother about the interview, the date, and the sex too. June was no prude. Having stayed single after her husband left her, she was no stranger to one-night flings and considered herself a modern woman.

"The date was so amazing. But then today was just, I don't know. Do all guys drink that much?"

"Sweetheart." June reached over the dinner plates and grabbed her daughter's hand. "What it sounds like to me is that this guy has a little too much affection for the drink. I would advise you to tread lightly, be careful. Remember what it was like for us?"

"He's not like dad, Mom." Iris pulled her hand away and crossed her arms over her chest, perturbed that her mom could even suggest such a thing.

"I'm not saying that. I'm just saying be careful. Red flags are not to be ignored. I'm only trying to help."

"Yeah... I know. Thanks, Mom."

ELEVEN

Elijah sat on a barstool at The Tavern and held a whiskey neat in his hand while he scoped out the scene. His eyes landed on a pair of young women in tight skirts, at the end of the bar. He swallowed the last sip of this drink and broke away from his group of artists and employees surrounding him. He made his way to the girls, their eyes fluttered at him while their lips smiled seductively, inviting him over.

"Ladies. Can I buy you a drink?" The women gave their assent, and Elijah nodded to the bartender, who complied with a silent understanding and poured three whiskeys. Small talk followed, and then another drink. Several drinks later, Elijah lost all inhibitions and didn't flinch when one of the girls rubbed his cheek and pulled him close to her mouth. She leaned in and whispered, "You wanna come with me to the bathroom really quick? I wanna show you something."

A half-smile graced his face, and he looked at her temptingly. She smiled back and led him through the bar and into the women's restroom.

The woman, still hardly more than a stranger, pushed

him into the stall and locked the latch. Hidden from peering eyes, she let loose on him, and he allowed her to take what she wanted. After two minutes of heavy petting, he got distracted by someone huffing in the next stall over. The sound was one he was all too familiar with—someone cutting and sniffing drugs. He laughed it off at first.

"Sounds like someone's having a better time than we are!" he said to the woman attached to his neck.

She laughed out loud and slammed her palm against the partition. "Hey, you gonna share?"

"Oh, no, no. Not for me. I'm good." Elijah said before the joke went any further.

"Sorry. This is some good shit, and I only got enough for me," said the voice on the other side. Elijah's eyes went wide as he recognized it.

"Mom?" Elijah shouted. Silence. "Get the fuck out here!" he shouted again, gently disconnecting himself from the new friend he'd made and exited the stall.

More silence.

"I can fucking see your feet. Open the fucking door. Now." Elijah grabbed the handle of the stall his mother was hiding in. He shook the thin metal door, nearly ripping it out from where it was bolted to the wall. The woman, who a second earlier was hanging off his body, yelped in fear and hurried out of the bathroom.

The toilet flushed. "Okay. Okay. Hold on. I'm pulling my pants up, honey, that's all." Marie's voice trembled.

"Oh, don't give me that shit. Come out. Now."

Marie emerged from the stall like a child who'd been caught with their hand in the cookie jar. Seeing red, Elijah grabbed her by the arm and escorted her out of the bathroom.

"What the fuck is wrong with you? I was right there!

Why do you think you can get away with this shit around me?" He dragged her through the bar and out into the parking lot.

The car ride home was silent, but once inside the safety of their home, he let all his rage and anger out on her like it had been bubbling up inside him all his life.

"You are a burden. I'm tired of having to rescue you from yourself. How many fucking times have I had to pull you out of a tent downtown with a needle in your arm? How many times have I sent you to rehab? You told me you wanted to get better, so why aren't you? It's always the same shit with you, over and over. Why do I have to be the mother? You're supposed to be the one taking care of me, but instead, I'm carrying you, and I always have, my whole fucking life!"

"I'm sorry, baby. Please. I'm sorry. I'll try to be better; I promise," Marie cried trying to plead with her son.

"No. I'm tired. I can't fucking do this with you anymore. Where'd you get the drugs? Do you still have any? Give them to me now." Elijah held out his hand as he towered over her. Marie cowered under his dominance and produced a small red balloon from her sock. She placed it in his palm and hid her head in her hands as she sobbed. As the item fell into his grasp, he softened. His chin quivered, and his eyes became wet. The thought of losing his mother haunted him.

"That's all I have, I swear."

"Mom." His voice cracked as emotion overwhelmed him. "You gotta stop this. Please. You're all I got. You're my mom, and I need you here."

"I'm so sorry, baby. I promise I'll do better." Marie hugged her son. He sank into her arms as they both broke down.

"I had a great time with Ma tonight," Elijah said after dinner with Iris' mom, June. He wasted no time adopting her as his own.

Dinner at June's house was always a special event. June made sure favorite meals and desserts were available, and the conversation was light and cheery.

"Yeah, Mom's the best," Iris said as they made the journey back to Iris' apartment.

"She's a cool old lady."

"Sorry, she made you fix her door. She does that every time I come over, making me step up on a ladder somewhere. Now that I have a boyfriend, I don't have to do that anymore!" Iris laughed and Elijah chuckled along with her.

"I don't mind. Makes me feel useful. That's how a mom is supposed to act with their adult children."

"Oh, good. I'm glad you think so because if we ever come over again, I can guarantee you she'll have something else for you to do."

"If?" Elijah looked at her with a question mark on his face.

"Yeah, I mean, if you want to, of course, you're welcome to, now that she knows you and likes you and you're handy."

"We should make it a regular thing. Every Wednesday night, dinner with Ma, and the doorknobs."

Iris felt her heart jump and swell inside its cage. "You really like my mom, don't you?"

Elijah shrugged. "She's nice. You know I don't exactly have the picture-perfect relationship with my mom."

Iris nodded and smiled, feeling like this was something of value she had to offer him. "It's settled then. Weekly dinners with Ma."

"And the doorknobs." Elijah winked.

Iris laughed. "Of course, the doorknobs."

It was a Sunday night, their first anniversary. Iris had closed the studio down. The plan was to meet Elijah at his place for dinner and spend a quiet evening together. Iris arrived at Elijah's apartment, expecting him there, waiting for her. She banged on the door, but there was no answer. After waiting and listening through the door for any sign of him inside, she called his phone. No answer. She gave up after several unanswered texts and phone calls, and went home to the apartment she shared with Sarah.

She cried on the drive home, angry and upset at having to go back to her own house with no Elijah. With every city block she passed, she felt a pullback in the opposite direction. An ache to be nearer to him grabbed her chest and squeezed.

When she walked in, she found Sarah sitting on the couch with a forlorn look, not wanting to say I told you so, but Iris could feel it in the air. Sarah hugged her as silent tears began falling out of Iris' eyes.

"What happened? Where is he?" Sarah asked when Iris was ready to talk about it.

Iris shrugged. "At the bar again, I guess."

Sarah rubbed her back. "You've been putting up with this for a year now. He's always at the fucking bar. Doesn't that remind you of anything? Anyone?"

A sharp look came into Iris' eyes. "He's not my father, okay? Just drop it already. I swear you and my mother are the same person."

AS IF SHE were moving through the stages of grief, Iris' dejection turned to anger and she began pacing around her bedroom. Minutes passed, and she checked her phone obsessively, calling, and leaving voicemails. "It's our fucking anniversary, Elijah. Where are you? Call me back!" She sent the same voicemail over and over as if repeating herself would force him to comply. But all it did was fuel the fire in her belly that bubbled into a rage.

"Hey." Sarah peeked into Iris' room. Iris was standing, unable to relax or put down her phone. "I'm going out with a few people from work. You wanna come with us?" The offer, meant to distract, fell on deaf ears.

"Huh?" Iris responded, without looking up for her phone. "He's gonna call back, I know he will. He always does."

"Okay, well, if you change your mind, we'll be at the Cantina."

"Yeah, yeah. Thanks. Have a good night!" Iris had no intention of leaving her post. She would wait for Elijah like she always did.

IT WAS two in the morning when he finally replied to her with a simple text message.

Home. Come thru.

Still awake, she hurried to heed his call. She barreled through the empty road, marched up to his apartment, and banged on the front door.

"What the hell, Elijah? Where have you been? I've been calling you all night!"

"I'm sorry. I got the dates mixed up. I thought you were coming over tomorrow," he said, opening the door.

"That's bullshit, Elijah. I reminded you today at the studio that it was our anniversary and you promised me a special night." Iris stood cross-armed in the living room.

"Oh..." He paused. "Well, it is a special night. I have something for you, actually."

Iris wasn't convinced, her face held a scowl and her shoulders remained tense. He pulled out his key ring and removed his house key.

"Here." He handed it to her. "I've been thinking about it a lot lately, and I think I'm ready for you to move in. I like you being here when I get home and I want this to be our place."

"What?" Iris' voice dropped to a whisper, and her glare softened to a gaze. She held her hand up over her mouth as her eyes filled with tears. "You want me to move in?" she said, making sure she hadn't imagined the question.

"Yeah, I do. If you move in, you'll always be here and you won't have to worry about where I am or what I'm doing cause you'll know I'm always coming home to you."

Iris melted into a proverbial puddle. Any anger or frustration she'd felt instantly dissipated. She let out a cry that became laughter, releasing all tension and filling her with dopamine-fuel euphoria.

"Happy anniversary." Elijah pulled her to him, kissed her, and guided her to the bedroom.

IRIS WASTED NO TIME. She took the next day off work to pack up and move into Elijah's apartment. There was a sense of accomplishment with each delicately wrapped plate or vase stuffed into a box. This was it. It was happening. Things would be different now.

"Iris. Are you absolutely sure you want to do this?" Sarah gave one final plea. Iris didn't say a word; it would only make it harder for her to leave.

"Think about what you're doing, Iris. He's an alcoholic, he's never even told you he loves you. Is this really what you want?"

"Sarah!" Iris dropped the box at her feet. "I know he loves me, okay. He doesn't have to say it. He shows me every day."

Sarah held her hands up in surrender. Her soft voice reached out to offer one final piece of advice. "Iris... I just want you to be happy. If you think this is right for you, maybe it is. But, you're always welcome back here, whenever you need it. Okay?"

"I won't need it, but thanks. See you Friday for Marg Meetup!"

Elijah knocked on June's door. She'd called him over unexpectedly to help her with a few things around the house. It wasn't Wednesday, no dinner planned, but Elijah was happy to help. The two of them had developed a strong bond over the year, and June had adopted him as a son.

"Elijah! Hi, sweetheart. Come in."

"Hey, Ma!" The two hugged, and Elijah scraped his boots on the welcome mat before walking inside.

"So, moving in? That's a big step! You sure you're ready for that?"

Elijah laughed nervously and rubbed the back of his neck. "You know, you've got a good one there, Ma. She's a good girl. You two have both been so good to me. I feel like part of the family. Moving in seemed like the next natural step."

June went to fetch a tool belt and motioned to Elijah to follow her through the house. She pointed at burned lightbulbs that needed changing and a stuck bathroom drawer that needed adjustment.

"And the drinking? Can't be out all hours of the night at

the bar when your girlfriend is worried sick at home waiting for you, can you? A man needs to make sure his woman feels safe and secure."

"I know, I know. I'm working on that. I'm gonna try and be better."

June smiled, satisfied with his answer. "Well, I guess I'm glad to have you around. Iris has never taken to a man quite like she's taken to you. Not sure if that's a good thing or not. You do remind me a bit of her father."

"I'm not like him, Ma. I could never hurt her as he did. I had a deadbeat dad too. I know what that feels like, and I'm not that man."

June nodded. "Okay, well. As long as you treat my daughter right, and get a handle on the drinking, I'm happy to have you with us. It's been just the two of us for so long."

Elijah looked back at her and smiled as he twisted a fresh lightbulb into the empty socket over his head. "Anything else around here I can do for you?" June flapped her wrist and shook her head. She thanked him for coming and sent him away with a batch of fresh-baked cookies.

* * *

ELIJAH MUNCHED on the cookies as he drove away and thought about his life, the choices he'd made, and how he got to where he was. He recognized the value of having a woman like Iris love him and a mother like June to replace the mess of a mother that birthed him. Right there, over a bite of oatmeal chocolate chip, he resolved that he would be a good man to Iris. The drinking would stop, the late nights at the bar were over, and the flirting with other women, no more.

He was going to try, for the first time in his life, to be the man he'd always dreamed he could be. He'd never had a proper role model to show him how, but how hard could it be? The checklist in his head made it sound easy. No drinking, check. No late nights, check. No more girls in bar bathrooms, check. He hurried home to help Iris settle into their new life together.

Marie was a project. A child Elijah kept close and protected from the allure of the pills that called to her from the dark alleyways and tent-lined streets of The Tenderloin. She became a spot of contention for Iris and Elijah and the reason they fought, despite Elijah having remained sober and his alcoholism no longer having a role.

"Baby, can you spot me some walk-around money?" Marie asked her son, nothing unusual. Iris watched the interaction and stood in the background, waiting for Elijah to stand up to her and tell her no.

"Mom, you just got paid three days ago. What do you need money for now?"

"Oh, nothin' baby, I just wanna walk around town, maybe get my nails done, lunch?"

"Iris will take you to get your nails done. You don't need money for that."

"Oh no, I don't wanna be a bother. Cash is fine."

"Okay, here. Just go." Elijah let out a frustrated sigh and gritted his teeth as he pulled twenty dollars from his wallet and shoved it in her direction. "But you're taking Iris with you!"

"Thanks, baby!" Marie grabbed the bill with a quick strike of her wrist and half-skipped out of the studio.

Iris approached Elijah. "Why do you give her the money? You know what she wants it for. She doesn't want to go out with me to get her nails done. She's bullshitting you!"

"Don't tell me how to deal with my mother, Iris. Just go with her, hurry, I don't want her out alone this late."

"Oh, and you're okay with me going out late, knowing where she's going? She's going to get drugs, Elijah. Why should I have anything to do with that? She couldn't care less if she got herself killed. You want me to walk into a murder tent with her?"

"Shut the fuck up, Iris," Elijah screamed and threw his blowpipe on the ground. It crashed on the concrete and reverberated with the clanging sound of hollow metal. Iris startled at the noise and jumped in place. "Fuck this. Lock up. I'm out." Elijah removed his gloves and walked out, leaving Iris still standing there in shock.

"Oh, so you're just gonna walk away then? Just leave me here?" Iris' voice became louder with every step he took away from her.

"I can't do this with you right now. I need a drink. Go home, Iris. I'll be home later."

"Oh, yeah, great. So, we're back to this? Another fun-filled night of Elijah getting drunk while Iris waits patiently at home. Perfect!" The sarcasm was lost in the open air as Elijah refused to stop his pursuit out the door.

"You better not tell Ma about this. I'll be home later. Just chill."

Iris stood still and watched him go. "Don't tell Ma?" Iris

said to herself under her breath. "You mean *MY* mom? Because your own is such a fuckup?" Silent tears streamed down her face as she pulled her phone from her back pocket to make a call.

"Hello?" June's soft voice answered.

"Mom?" Iris' heartache was apparent in her tone as words blubbered out of her. "He left again. He's gone. I don't know what to do anymore."

"Oh, my sweet girl. I'm so sorry. Tell me what happened?" Moments like these it was her mother she needed.

"His stupid mom." Tears made her words choppy. "She's always trying to get high, and Elijah knows it, but it's like he can't say no to her." The heaving in her chest made her take long pauses in the middle of her sentences.

"Sweetheart, listen. I know you love Elijah, and I love him like a son too, I do, but you know how difficult he has it with his mom. She's an addict, and the hardest thing in the world is loving an addict."

"Yeah, tell me about it. Elijah's on his way to the bar, four years of sobriety, gone."

"Oh, honey. He's done so well over these years. Something must have been bubbling up. But I know. He has his demons. Sweetheart, you have to decide if this is really what you want. There's a real possibility that he's never gonna change, you see that, don't you?"

"But I love him, Mom."

"Oh, I know you do. But if he's slipping again, who knows what this could mean?"

Iris let out an extended sigh before answering. "Yeah..." She wiped the left-over tears from her face.

"Okay, well... Why don't you come over here tonight and have a sleepover? I'll get your favorite ice cream."

"Yeah, I guess." Iris sniffled and took a breath.

"Great. Girl's night. Okay, honey. I'm gonna go to the store and I'll see you soon?"

"Okay, bye."

GIRLS' night with Mom offered little relief. Iris spent the evening obsessing over her phone, waiting for a call or text message that would ask her to come home. But it never did. An uncomfortable anxiety, all too familiar, crept up inside. Mother and daughter made the best of it. They talked and ordered pizza and later ate their ice cream while watching a sappy romcom.

"Have you talked to anyone at all about your relationship with Elijah?" Her mom asked.

"What? Like a professional? Mom, I can't do that." Iris sunk her head into her hands, deflated.

"Well, you know I love Elijah, and I want the best for you both, but..."

"But nothing!" Iris cut her mom off with a harsh turn of voice. "I love him, Mom. I can't let him go." The mood turned somber and the air thickened with tension. Her mother shut her eyes, taking a moment before responding.

"Look, Iris, I know you've always taken issue with your father not being around, but this is exactly why I let him go, so you wouldn't grow up to see him treat me the way Elijah treats you. I thought that would stop you from tolerating a man like him. Being sober for a little while means nothing if he's just gonna go right back to the bottle when things get tough." Her mother's voice rose as she spoke until she became so hot, her face became bright red, and the veins in her neck stuck out.

Iris broke down in tears and covered her face as she sat there on the couch, a half-eaten bowl of ice cream resting in her lap. Her mother's anger had startled her, taking her back in time to the young girl who hid in her spot while her parents yelled. "I just want him to be better," she sobbed.

"Well, for your sake, I do, too. This isn't what I want for you," June said, frowning.

Iris arrived back at the apartment she shared with Elijah early the next morning, leaving her mother's house before she had woken up. She hadn't slept well that night. The blue glow of her cell phone kept her engaged waiting for the response that never came.

Elijah was fast asleep in their bed. The sight of him relieved her; she could breathe again. Too wired for TV or a quiet breakfast, she tidied up a bit to help herself relax. She grabbed the rags and cleaning products from under the sink. She reached deep into the cabinet and heard a strange clinging sound. A closer look behind the Pledge and Clorox revealed crushed beer cans, an empty whiskey bottle, and a half-eaten jar of peanut butter. She shook her head and rolled her eyes as she mumbled to herself. "Who the hell does he think he's hiding from? Great hiding spot, Elijah, right where I keep all the cleaning supplies that I use all the time... idiot."

Iris pursed her lips and groaned, gathering the trash. She tossed the cans in the garbage with a gentle arm, not wanting to risk disturbing Elijah's sleep.

With a quiet fire in her step, she moved through the apartment, picking up strewn clothing and replacing misplaced items. She sprayed the surfaces and struck the rag across like she was combing knots out of a horse's mane. She shook her head at the crusted, dried puke stains that covered the toilet bowl. "Ugh, disgusting." She scrubbed hard and let her frustrations out into the bowl. It had been years since she'd had to clean up after one of Elijah's benders; it was a feeling she didn't miss.

She looked for the laundry in the darkness of their bedroom, and as she collected and separated the garments, he stirred in the sheets. It wasn't only stiff sheets she heard crackling in his movements, but also the sound of liquid sloshing against glass walls. In a huff, she marched to the bed and ripped back his covers to reveal, curled in his embrace, a half-empty bottle of his favorite dark liquor, and she saw red.

"Elijah!" she screamed as she stood over his naked body.

He startled awake. "What... the fuck, Iris? I'm sleeping," he said, growling as he pulled a pillow over his head.

"What the fuck is this?" She grabbed the bottle and shook it in front of his covered face.

"Oh, my god. Would you get off my fucking back!" he yelled back at her. "You were being a bitch yesterday, so I went out and had a few drinks. Jesus!"

"A few drinks? A few drinks isn't hiding empty beer cans and jars of peanut butter in a cabinet... or puking all over the toilet. You're drunk, all your progress down the drain. You're no better than your drug addict mother."

"Shut the fuck up!" he screamed so loud a framed photo of them at the beach rattled in its place above their bed. His face turned red, and his chest rose and fell fast with his breathing. He screamed again, this time without words, and threw the half-empty bottle of alcohol at Iris' head. He missed, hitting the wall with such force, the bottle broke into shards, shanks, and pieces of wet dust. The sound of shattering glass echoed through the room. Iris screamed, covered her head with her hands, and fell to her knees.

Her mother was huddled on the floor over her daughter's small body. A raging husband punched mirrors, threw vases, and flipped furniture like a tornado. The two frightened bodies trembled on the floor, at the mercy of the powerful man that dominated the room. Violence poured out of him. The sight of his woman and daughter cowering before him was of no consequence to his actions, except perhaps fueling him to continue. Little Iris focused her eyes on the dingy yellow wallpaper, trying to block her fear.

Iris remained on the floor, rocking back and forth, a desperate attempt to comfort herself and pull out of the memory. Elijah's voice was the only thing that could break through it.

"I'm sorry, I'm sorry." Elijah got up from the bed and knelt beside Iris. He reached out for her. She shivered at his touch. "I'm sorry, please. I didn't mean it."

"You never do..."

He pulled her into him and embraced her with his brawny arms, kissing her forehead. Triggered by his touch, her neck and shoulders tensed. "I didn't mean it. I'm so sorry for scaring you." He held her tight as she cried into his arms. "I'm so sorry, Iris. Please forgive me?" He begged and groveled until the tension released its hold on her, and she warmed to his touch.

"I love you too," she said between sobs, responding to a statement he hadn't made, and hugged him back. She smiled, letting him know the fight was over and they could move on to the next step in their pattern—making up. He smiled back, taking the cue.

SEVENTEEN

Iris found the strength to lift herself off the floor. The mess of broken glass glittered under the ceiling light, and the stench of whiskey swirled around the room. She went to the kitchen to fetch the broom and dustpan. As she made her way to the utility closet, she heard a familiar tune. The melodic voice of Britney Spears stimulated her eardrums and brought to her face a wide smile and soft eyes. She walked back into the bedroom, broom, and dustpan in hand, her smile becoming larger with each step.

There he was, Elijah, dancing and singing along like the first time all those years ago. He exaggerated his hip thrusts and neck wobbles. He rolled his eyes and stuck out his tongue, mocking the gesture they once thought was cool. Iris laughed out loud as a single tear streamed down her cheek.

"What are you doing?" She asked, shouting to be heard over the music, her voice full of mirth.

"Shhhh..." he said as he held his index finger up to his lips and looked at her, eyes lighting up. "Don't speak, just let it take you."

Iris kept laughing. "You're crazy!"

"Come here, girl." He grabbed her hips and pulled her into him. He guided her through a flamboyant dance routine that last the entire song. That same electric feeling she had felt the first night they met came rushing back and her heart flooded with expectations of what a rosy future with this man might look like.

The song ended, but he continued to hold her, keeping his eyes locked on hers.

"You know I care about you, right?"

"Yeah…" She wasn't sure where this was going, he'd never spoken to her in such a serious tone before.

"I know you put up with a lot for me, and my mom, and just all of it. I want you to know that this is real for me. And I'm prepared to make a real commitment to you."

Iris' throat clogged. She took a giant gulp as her eyes widened.

Standing before her in his boxer briefs, he reached behind his back and into his waistband, pulling out a small black box. With the box in hand, he dropped to one knee. Iris gasped and brought both hands to her mouth. She squeezed her eyes shut, letting tears fall freely down her face.

"Girl, you better look at me when I do this!" She choked on a giggle and took a deep breath before her body froze. "I want you to know that I'm here. I've always been here, and I always will be. I want you to be my wife." He presented the little black box to her that held a diamond ring. It sparkled in the reflection of her glistening eyes.

Iris, still frozen, couldn't speak, couldn't breathe, and only nodded as he smiled and arose. The couple embraced and kissed. Iris let out a few joyful cries that turned into deep breaths of air.

"I can't believe this. Are you for real?" She finally said as he slipped the ring onto her finger.

"I am for real. I want you, I want us, and I love that you love me. This is gonna be the rest of our lives."

"I love you too, Elijah." Once again, she responded to a statement he hadn't actually made. The phrase *I love you* never left his lips. But Iris didn't notice. She paused to admire the new sparkle on her hand.

"Oh no. I forgot to ask Ma." Elijah let out a groan as he threw his head back and covered his face with his hands.

"Oh, you're in trouble now," Iris teased. "It's fine, don't worry. We're going over for dinner Wednesday, anyway, it'll be a nice surprise for her."

"Great, but first, you are definitely getting a manicure if you're gonna be showin' off that ring."

Iris chuckled. "I know, I know. Nothing worse than dirty fingernails." She playfully bumped into him, grabbed his collar, and pulled him in for a kiss.

"Hi, Ma!" Elijah greeted June as the door opened.

"Hi, sweetheart, how are you?" She accepted Elijah's hug before hugging Iris. "Come in, come in."

"I hope you guys are hungry. We have a smorgasbord." June pointed to the dining room table full of various meats and cheeses, crackers, olives, and chocolates. "I've also made spaghetti, meatballs, garlic bread, chicken curry, samosas, and enchiladas."

"Wow! You weren't kidding," said Iris.

"Well..." June waved her hands and shook her head. "I wanted to make everyone's favorite. Elijah's got such an eclectic taste. I didn't forget anything, did I?"

"No, Ma. You got it all... It's a perfect night for a feast. Iris and I have some news."

"Oh?" June turned her head to the side and opened her eyes.

"We're engaged!" Elijah said the words, and Iris presented her hand with a toothy smile and sparkle in her eyes.

"Oh. Oh, oh my!" June cupped her hands over her

mouth, then grabbed both of them in a firm embrace. "How exciting. Oh, my god. I can't believe it."

Iris and Elijah laughed, all three of them relishing the moment.

"Champagne. We need champagne." Ma hurried off to the kitchen. "I have a bottle somewhere," she shouted.

"Here, let me help you, Ma," Elijah said as he went off after her while Iris sauntered over to the table of starters. A toast followed. Their glasses bubbled as they held them high and clinked them together in celebration of the moment.

Dinner was polite and fun. They spoke about the wedding, details of arrangements they would make. June knew a caterer that would be perfect for the occasion. Iris mentioned it would be beautiful to hold the ceremony in the studio, surrounded by colorful glass sculptures and the warm glow of the glass furnaces. Elijah agreed with everything while indulging in the scrumptious feast.

Elijah patted his stomach, sitting back in his chair, and threw his arm around Iris. "That was some damn good cookin', Ma. You're the best."

"Oh." June waved away the compliment. "I'll just clean up. You go relax in the living room. Iris, will you help me with these dishes?"

"Sure." Iris stood and began gathering dishes with June while Elijah went into the living room.

Once in the kitchen and away from his view, June's eyes changed and turned sharp.

"Iris, what are you doing?" Her voice matched her face.

"What are you talking about?" The change of tone confused her.

"Iris, you were just over here last night crying to me about him. He's fallen off the wagon. I thought we talked about this. Now you're engaged?" June threw her hands up.

"Mom..." Iris averted her eyes from her mother's scowl. "I love him, and he loves me. And he loves you more than his own mother."

"Yes, of course. I love Elijah. He's a sweet boy when he's around, but he's troubled. A married man shouldn't be throwing fits and going out to bars at all hours of the night."

"Don't you remember what it was like for you in the beginning? It was so easy for him to fall back into those habits. One bad fight about his mom was all it took."

Iris' eyes welled up and her lips quivered. She dropped the first load of dishes in the sink and turned on the faucet. Tension released into the sponge as she applied pressure to each dish with every scrub. June stood over her with crossed arms, not finished with the point she was making.

"Look, I just don't want to see you get hurt."

"You literally jumped up and down and congratulated us with champagne. What the hell was all that about?" Iris squeezed the water from the sponge and clenched her teeth.

"I don't know. I don't know why I did that... Maybe because you're so damn sensitive when it comes to him. Maybe because you're my child and he's not, and I don't want to react in front of him. I don't want to be in the middle of one of your fights. You're the one who needs to make this decision, not me. You got yourself into this mess of a relationship."

"And the truth finally comes out. All this 'it's ok, sweetheart, let me help you' bullshit was always just that, right? Bullshit. You're so two-faced. You can't be supportive and loving one second and then completely flip the next. You don't love Elijah, do you? You just don't want conflict."

June scoffed and rolled her eyes. Iris turned back to the sink, grabbed a dish, but it slipped out of her hands and cracked in half. Both women jumped from the sound of shattering ceramic.

"You two okay in there?" Elijah called from the living room.

"Fine. We're fine, just dropped a dish," Iris called back, forcing a smile and trying to appear casual. "Tell him. Go on." She dropped the fake smile as she addressed her mother. "Tell him how you feel, break his heart just like you've broken mine."

"Iris, this isn't about how I feel about him. This is about how you truly feel about him, behind this wall of insecurity that makes you believe you love him."

Little Iris watched out the window as her father got in his car and drove away. Not even a "goodbye" or a "see ya later, kid." At seven years old, she was fatherless, abandoned, and alone. She cried, harder and harder as the taillights dimmed in the growing distance until they were gone.

Her tears faded away and were replaced by water pouring from the faucet as she came back into the kitchen, staring blankly at the sink of dirty dishes, a broken piece still in her hand.

"I love you, Iris, and if you feel I have failed you because I have been too supportive of this fantasy relationship of yours, then for that, I am sorry. But you are an adult, and it's time to stop playing pretend. Wake up!" June plastered a fake smile on her face and walked over to the fridge. "Who wants pie?" she said walking to the living room, ending the conversation with Iris, and resuming the show.

"Oh, yeah. That sounds great, Ma. Can I help?" Elijah said, rising from the couch. Iris stayed standing, in a cast of stone at the sink. "Hey? You okay?"

"Huh?" Iris snapped back into herself when she heard him call. "Yeah, I'm fine. Just trying to get this broken dish out of the way." She turned off the faucet and smiled her way over to the trash where she dropped the broken piece of plate, feeling like she was tossing in a broken piece of her heart.

"Can you grab the pie server from that drawer over there?" June said, pointing to a kitchen drawer.

"Oh, sure." Elijah rifled through the drawer and pulled out the shiny metal utensil and handed it to June. "Here you go, Ma. What kind of pie are we having?"

"I got your favorite, German Chocolate."

"Perfect. Love you, Ma." Elijah chuckled, June smiled, and Iris observed the interaction with newfound skepticism.

"Now eat up," June said as she handed him a large slice of pie.

The breakup text came abruptly. Like Iris had been living in a fantasy, she reflected and couldn't see the events that might lead to something like this. It made no sense. It couldn't be real. Instead, she held strongly, almost chokingly, to her faith in Elijah, using the ring on her finger as his testament to a higher commitment.

It was Friday, and Iris was alone again. Spending her evenings alone had become common since the engagement. Like a dance she let him lead her on. Would he come in with flowers and big apologies? Would he have an excuse? Would he come home at all?

Flustered, she sat on a crushed green velvet sofa in their living room. She'd begged Elijah to buy it for her when she'd moved in. Mid-century modern was the posh style, and she'd wanted their life together to begin surrounded by beautiful things. She filled the apartment with straight armchairs and tables with angled legs. Having a put-together apartment meant she had a put relationship. In her head, it made sense.

Her anxiety manifested into a sensation of ants

crawling under her skin. She could no longer sit still or resist the temptation to call. Where was he? Who was he with? When was he coming home?

When her phone pinged, her screen lighting up with a message from Elijah, she nearly jumped from her velvet perch. Not knowing what to expect, her hands trembled as she read the text.

I'm not coming home tonight. I'm removing myself from the lease. See you Monday.

This was not part of the dance. Iris' eyes widened as a lump grew in her throat. She shook her head, laughed out loud, and shivered as a lightning bolt of rage coursed through her. Her hands were shaking too much to type, so she called instead. No answer. Again, again, again. Each call met with nothing.

"You fucking coward!" she screamed.

She slumped back down into the couch, trying to find an ounce of comfort, squirming in vain. "This stupid fucking couch," she shouted. "I hate it!" as if yelling at the couch-together removed the blame from herself and placed it somewhere less damning.

Iris tossed and turned through the night, unable to find sleep or rest. The ceiling and blank sections of walls held her gaze. Staring at them, she tried to convince herself he would be back. Of course, he would, she reasoned. They work together; they live together, they're engaged... that couldn't all mean nothing. Tomorrow would be better. She lulled her into a false sense of security, she dreamed of a future where they lived, together, in love, and happy.

THE NEXT MORNING, she called, no answer. She shook it off because it was easier to pretend nothing was wrong, that he was just out being Elijah, on another bender. As long as he didn't answer, she could tell herself that he would come home.

By Sunday, there was still no sign of him and something inside her snapped. In a fit of panic, she tore through the apartment. Every crevice was inspected. She'd stumbled across hidden beer cans before, there must be something more to clue her in to where he was or why he was leaving her. Without knowing what she was looking for, she hunted for it all the same.

The apartment looked like someone had broken in but hadn't taken anything—drawers rifled through, cabinets opened, and contents removed, closets ransacked, clothes strewn across the floor, cushions, pillows, and blankets tossed into piles where they did not belong.

All to find... Nothing. Not a single letter or receipt or photo existed that brought her any solace. Iris stood in her living room with her hands on her hips and soaked in the mess she'd created. She dropped to the floor, distressed at the thought of cleaning up when her eyes fell onto a shiny glass screen hiding underneath the TV console. She pulled the object from the dark space. An iPad.

Wasting no time, she typed in a four-digit code on the lock screen. Success, access granted. She scrolled through his private emails, phone records, photos, and text messages. What she found broke her heart into smaller and smaller pieces until she was left with nothing but red dust at her feet.

His call logs, messages, and emails were filled by a woman he'd named *sexy*. She searched through the photos and found several lewd pictures of her breasts, ass, and more. But none that showed the "other woman's" face. She was everywhere, the first text message between them having happened the night before their engagement, the night Elijah started drinking again.

Iris broke into tears as the gravity of this realization set in. She blamed alcohol for his actions that had now sent her world crashing down around her.

Iris opened an email, the subject line read: *Our New Forever.*

"Hey Sexy," the email began. "I know we've only known each other a couple weeks, but life with you has been everything I've been missing. I can't wait to go away with you. Tickets are booked and we're good to go! I'm gonna tell her tomorrow. Then it's just you and me and our new forever."

She put the iPad down and sat in her own nothingness, only the sound of her breath cutting through the silence. She didn't know how to react. Elijah was not coming home, and she was alone, abandoned again. She had knots in her stomach and felt pressure in her pelvis. Cramps. Unable to confront the new information, she opened her phone to check her period tracker app. The calendar revealed she had missed her period by two weeks. "How..." she said out loud and put on her shoes, grabbed her keys, and headed out the door.

She arrived at the local pharmacy's family planning section where various brands of home pregnancy tests called out to her like tiny voices in her head screaming "Pick me! Pick me!"

She stepped out of the bathroom in silence and reflected on her last moments with him. The air was quiet, the light was dim, and the reality of the positive pregnancy test she'd just taken weighed down on her. Her mind was fuzzy and she could hear static ringing in her ears.

It was Sunday evening. She only had to get through one more week at the studio until she and her mother planned to go away on a girls' weekend at the Bay. The getaway she needed. It would be an escape from the glum reality of single life, a distraction from the nagging in her brain that made her think about what he was doing with the other woman. June wouldn't let her obsess over social media as she did during the lonely evening hours she spent in her apartment with no one to stop her.

But hope had her convinced that once he found out about the baby, everything could be okay. Monday she would tell him. She imagined the scenario playing out in her head—he would come back to her, graveling, and she would forgive him. Together they would find a way for him to stop drinking, again, and this would all go away.

The images of the other woman played like a morbid slideshow in her head. She sat on the couch and scrolled through her feed. There were no new pictures of Elijah since the last time she'd checked. She was so immersed in her stalking that the knock on her door startled her out of the couch.

Her heart beat faster as she took shallow steps toward the door.

"Oh, hey, Mom. What are you doing here?" Her body relaxed as she moved aside to let June in.

"Hi, sweetie, I'm sorry. I just wanted to check in, see how you're doing. I got your text last night, and I wanted to make sure everything was ok."

"Yeah, I'm fine, I'm just... hangin' out."

"I can see that," June said as her eyes scanned the apartment, still in shambles. "Why don't you let me help you clean up a bit?"

"No, Mom. I'm fine. I don't need help. I've just been busy."

"Okay, well, sit down with me for a bit. Come talk to me." June led them both to the living room. Iris broke down and fell into her mother's lap.

"I just can't believe he's gone, Mom. I'm alone. I'm all alone. I don't know what to do." The tightness in her throat made it hard to speak, but she got enough words out.

"I know, sweetie. I'm sorry. But maybe it's time to move on, sweetheart."

"I can't move on," Iris looked into her mother's eyes. "He's coming back. He has to."

"Oh, honey, I don't think..."

"Mom, I'm pregnant!"

June sat in silent shock until her brows furrowed. "That's impossible. I don't believe it."

"What do you mean you don't believe it? I'm telling you." Iris found the strength to stand from her crumpled position.

"Honey, I think you need to get some rest. You're stressed, and this has all been a little too much for you. But you can't be pregnant, he's..."

"Here, hold on!" Iris rushed to the bathroom to retrieve the evidence. She came rushing back into the living room, holding it out at chest level and presented it to June. "Look, see, right there, now do you believe me?"

"Iris, honey, you need to calm down right this instant!" June was shouting now. "You're not pregnant. You're stressed. But you need to get it together, now. This is not healthy."

"Look, just look at the test!"

"Iris, stop shouting!" June's face turned red. She grabbed Iris by the shoulders and shook her.

"You don't believe me? Why don't you believe me?"

"Iris!"

The women screamed, becoming louder and louder as they tried to get each other to listen. Adrenaline shot through Iris' head, and she pulled, trying to get away from her mother's grasp. She wanted to run, but there was nowhere to go. Calling upon her latent strength, she freed one arm and accidentally knocked over a glass vase Elijah had made for her as an anniversary present, sending it shattering to the ground.

There was a shrill and frightened scream. The sound of breaking glass echoed through the house as little Iris held her hands over her ears. Her father stood tall over June on the floor, shards of a broken mirror around her body. June turned to face little Iris, blood falling from her face, but holding a forced smile.

"It's okay, sweetie. Daddy didn't mean it. Mommy's okay."

Little Iris screamed and cried and moved to cuddle up to her mother. Pieces of glass broke into her skin as she crawled into her mother's embrace.

Iris froze and looked at June.

"Please, just calm down, sweetie." June's voice was sweet, calm, and collected.

"I'm sorry, I'm sorry." Iris took deep breaths in and out, fast and hard.

"It's okay. It's just a vase. We're okay... Come here, honey." Iris went to her mother and collapsed into her warm embrace. "There you go, sweetie. It was just an accident. We're okay; everything's okay." Her mother rocked her in her arms, the two women surrounded by tiny little pieces of colorful broken glass. Iris' breathing slowed and normalized.

"I'm sorry, Ma. I didn't mean to scare you. I've just been keyed up lately."

"I know, sweetie, it's okay. I'm here now. Come, sit down with me. Tell me what's going on with this pregnancy test."

"Nothing. It's exactly what it says it is. We were together until a couple of days ago, and here we are."

"Are you going to tell him about it?"

"I have to. It's his baby!"

"Okay, well, you take your time, and think about it clearly. I'm here for whatever you need, always, okay?"

"Yeah, I know. Thanks, Ma."

Iris let her mother help her clean the apartment. The broken glass was the first to go.

Iris made it to Friday. Even though Elijah hadn't shown up at the studio all week, she was still looking forward to girls' weekend with Ma. She left the office early that day, closed up, and hurried home to gather her things and head over so they could beat rush hour traffic. When her phone rang, she assumed it would be Ma, calling to ask where she was, if she was on her way, and to hurry. Ma was predictable in that way. "I'm going as fast as I can, Ma!" she answered without preamble. But the voice on the other end of the line was of the last person she'd expected to hear from.

"Hey, Iris... It's me, Sarah." Sarah was calm and submissive.

"Uh, hi." Disarmed by her softness, Iris relaxed her face and opened her heart. The two hadn't spoken much in the years since Iris first moved out of their shared apartment to be with Elijah. They had never gone to another Marg MeetUp, and their relationship fell into a casual acquaintanceship on social media. Likes and occasional hearts, now and again, replaced the need for words. Iris hadn't even mentioned the breakup to Sarah. Partly because she was still in denial that it was happening, but also because she didn't know how to frame it in a way that would come across as positive through a public social feed.

"Yeah, sorry to bombard you like this," said Sarah. "I just, I don't know, I miss you. I don't know where we went wrong or how we let our relationship just fall apart like this."

"I miss you too, Sarah. It's so funny, you must be in my head or something cause I was just thinking about you this morning." Iris laughed, diffusing the seriousness of the interaction. "I'm so glad you called though. I have a lot to tell you."

"Oh? Gush!"

Like no time had passed, the two of them were back to being as thick as they ever had been. Iris realized there was never any reason they shouldn't have been, and she was happy to have her friend close again.

"He left me. It finally happened." The words spilled out of her and with them an overflow of emotion. She sobbed, choked on the tears, and felt her body sink into her seat.

"Oh, my god, Iris. I'm so sorry. I... I don't know what to say. Can I help you with this? Will you let me?' Sarah offered her thoughts and her sympathy.

Iris let out a loud groan as she stuffed up her expression. "No, no. Thank you, but no. I just need to—" Iris was cut off by the ding of another call coming in. "Hold on. Ma's calling me."

"Ma? Elijah really rubbed off on you, huh?"

Iris rolled her eyes and scoffed. "Yeah, I guess... anyway, she's waiting for me, but, um, I don't wanna go yet."

"Well, you wanna come meet me for Marg MeetUp? Like old times? You can invite June too. I'd love to see her."

Beep... Beep... Beep. Another call from June interrupted them, but the alert went ignored.

"Oh, I would love to, but actually we have plans. We're doing a girls' trip to the Bay for the weekend." Iris paused before completing the thought. "Hey!" she said as a light-bulb had clicked on above her head, "speaking of old times, why don't you come with us? It'll be a classic girls' weekend like we had when we were teenagers!"

"Um, I mean... It's kinda last minute... but..."

"Come on, I miss you."

"Oh, what the hell, okay. Let me pack a bag really quick, and I'll meet you at June's?"

"Yes, okay, awesome, see you soon!"

THE SHORELINE WAS SCATTERED with bits of shells and land crabs that bubbled under the surface of the wet sand. The three women, together once again, sat on the beach and watched the sky as the last bit of sunshine fell behind the horizon.

"I'm not saying that what he did was even tolerable, it's despicable," Sarah started, "but, you mentioned that it happened right after he started drinking again. Maybe he found himself in a situation he didn't know how to deal with and maybe he pulled away from you out of shame? I see it a lot in my practice. That doesn't mean the relationship isn't salvageable. Just means he needs support."

Iris nodded as she reflected.

"Remember your father, Iris. There were plenty of nights he begged for forgiveness, down on his knees, and the next he'd be back to his shenanigans and taking it out on us. You remember."

Iris felt pulled in both directions. "Fine, I'm not saying we should get back together, but at least we all agree that he needs to know about the baby, right? And yes, I do remember my father. I remember that he left and that's not the life I want for my child. I have to tell him."

"Whatever you decide, sweetheart, you're not alone. Sarah and I will be there to support you at every turn. Always here for anything you need."

"We'll do it together. Just like we always did, since we were kids."

For the first time since the breakup, Iris felt a warmth inside her that rested like a cozy blanket around the most vulnerable pieces of her heart. She was not alone, and she felt love growing in her womb.

The end of the girl's weekend left Iris alone again with her thoughts. She spent the next several hours agonizing over the phone call she knew she had to make.

"Elijah, I'm pregnant. I'm sorry." She practiced her speech, fumbled over her words, and gently slapped herself in the head to get it right. "No. Damn it... Elijah, you're gonna be a dad! Yay! Ugh. No..."

The phone was in her hand. She clicked through her contacts, but before she could press the receiver icon, an incoming call came in, Elijah's face popped up on the screen. Without hesitating, she answered.

"Hi... I was just thinking about you. I have some news." Her voice was chipper, despite this being the first time she'd heard from him since his text message.

"They killed her; they got her."

"What? What's happening? Got who?" Iris' heart beat heavy in her chest.

"My mom. They got her, she's dead."

The weight of the news collapsed onto her shoulders like a cartoon anvil as she slunk to the floor. Her chest tightened and beads of sweat collected on her face and chest. "Your mom? How? When?" Iris' words were choppy and stagnated as she tried to breathe through the nightmare. Elijah was worse. He was hysterical, drowning his words in tears.

"They just said she's dead. She's gone. I don't know... Oh, my god, she's gone!"

"Elijah... I'm so, so sorry." She pulled her knees up to her body and rested her forehead on top of them. She held herself in a sitting fetal position and waited for him to say something.

Elijah sobbed. She let him for a while.

"What can I do for you, Elijah? Anything."

"I don't know. I need to find out what happened."

"How did you find out? Who told you?"

Elijah took another deep breath. "A detective called me just now. He said they found my mother's body, and I needed to go down to ID her, whatever that means. They found her in a dumpster with her head smashed in. It was a drug deal, I know it."

"Are you okay? Do you need me to come with you?"

"No, god no, I'm not gonna do that to you. But can you keep watching over the studio for a few more days while I handle everything?" He sounded somewhat put together like he was stitching himself up with thread but had poor needlepoint skills.

"Of course, don't worry about it. I'll take care of everything." It would be easy enough; she'd already been making excuses for him as to why he hadn't shown his face at work since the breakup.

"Cancel my studio sessions, call the Herman account and tell them..."

"You'll be late on the order. Of course. I got it. Don't even think about it."

"Thanks..." Elijah let out a sigh and cleared his throat. "What was it you wanted to tell me?"

"Huh? Oh, nothing. It can wait..."

"Okay, yeah, I'll call you. Thanks, I love you."

Iris gulped. "Love you too, talk to you soon." It was the first time he'd ever said those words to her. She grabbed onto the gesture, buried it deep inside her chest cavity, and used it to justify her feelings for him. He loved her as she'd always known, and finally, she had proof.

WITH A HEAVY HEART, Iris picked herself up, proceeded with overseeing the studio in Elijah's continued absence. Now was not the right time to bring up the pregnancy. Not while he was dealing with something so emotionally debilitating. The baby could wait. In the meantime, she would make herself available to Elijah and anything he needed.

Sarah was the next phone call she made.

"Oh, gosh. Let me know if there's anything I can do at all. Does he have a lawyer?"

"Oh, I don't think it's gotten to that point yet. We don't even know exactly what happened or what the police are looking for. Also, you should know... he said it. He finally told me he loves me. I always knew it, but he finally said the words."

"Wow. That's great, Iris. I mean, amid everything else, I'm glad he finally gave you that acknowledgment. We should talk about how you're feeling considering the circumstances."

Iris scoffed. "Okay, don't need you to put on your therapist hat, Sarah. I just wanted to mention it."

"What about you? Are you okay?"

"I'm... Uh..." Iris took a long pause. She felt horrible for Elijah, and couldn't imagine how painful and frightening Marie's death must have been, but her heart was still jumping from those three little words she'd waited so many years to hear. "I'm fine. Marie was always sweet to me, but I know she had problems. It's so horrible what's happened, but to be blunt, I can't say it's surprising. Poor woman." Iris tried hard to keep the perkiness from her voice; she couldn't wipe the smile from her face despite the tragedy.

"Well, listen, check in soon so I know you're still okay?"

"Yeah, I'll call you later."

"Okay, bye."

Iris wanted to believe she was okay, but soon the novelty of hearing *I love you* waned. An exhausting day with little sleep the night before had left her worn and overtired. She fell asleep only to wake up to the sound of her screams.

She had dreamed of Marie walking into a decrepit house filled with drugs and violent people engaging in despicable acts. Marie walked through the house, slowly and delicately on the floorboards, like a panther on the hunt. She wasn't looking for live prey; she was looking for a chemical catalyst to subdue her consciousness into a state of oblivion. Someone tossed pills to her. A dark shadow came up behind her and bludgeoned her to death with a glass statue that shattered as it met her skull. The sound of the breaking glass threw Iris into a fit as she thrashed in her sheets. It was a sound she was all too familiar with, one that ate up her childhood memories.

The image of Marie's face covered in blood and shards of glass was enough to wake her, chest heaving and sheets wet with sweat. From there, it was no use trying to sleep again. Terror accompanied every moment as the nightmares took her through to the morning sun.

At the studio, Monday, droopy eyes and a tired mind kept her from wanting to expend what little energy she'd left. She remained at her desk. The imagery she'd dreamed up occupied her waking hours as the sounds of shattering glass in the studio overtook her senses. Marie's bloody face flooded her mind.

"You okay? I heard a yelp," Jessica said as she poked her head into Iris' office.

"Yes, thank you." Iris took a breath and laughed. "Sorry, I guess I just scared myself. The glass. It's loud."

"The glass?" Jessica's face twisted into confusion. "You mean the crashing that literally happens twenty times a day? You sure you're okay?"

"Yeah, yeah. I know, it's silly. I didn't get a lot of sleep last night."

"You wanna go home and relax? I can lock up?"

"No, no. I'm fine. Thank you, Jessica."

By Friday, Marg MeetUp, Iris was desperate for a friend. Sarah would know what to do.

"Hi, yeah, can we get a pitcher of strawberry margarita? Two glasses, chips, and queso, thanks..." Sarah ordered for both of them as she always did.

"Uh, just one glass, please," Iris interjected.

"Oh yeah, duh!" Sarah laughed at herself.

Iris shook her head and rolled her eyes. "Just water for me. Thanks." The server nodded and walked away.

"So? Have you spoken to him yet?" Sarah leaned in and almost whispered her question.

"Well, no, obviously he's dealing with more important things right now..."

"Oh, my god. You're pregnant. How is that not the most important thing?" Sarah said.

"Shh." Iris held her finger over her mouth but smiled through the gesture. "Jesus, I don't think they heard you over at the other end of the bar. Wanna say it a little louder?"

"Sorry, sorry. But are you serious?"

"Come on, the guy's mom was just... you know. Don't you think I should give him some space to deal with that?"

"Ugh." Sarah slouched back in her chair. "It's been a week. You need to tell him."

"I want to, but right now just seems cruel."

"Alright, alright." Sarah raised her hands in a sign of submission. "What about-" Sarah cleared her throat, "what about the other woman?"

"I don't know. This whole thing is just so complicated. I'm so scared of doing this alone." Iris's eyes began to water, but she wiped them and crossed her arms, her chin quivering.

"Aw, honey." Sarah reached across the table for Iris' hand. "This is a lot, for anybody."

"Yeah, and it's not just the baby, I keep having these crazy nightmares. Like—" She stopped mid-speech, cocked her head, eyes locking intently on a flash of darkness in her peripheral vision.

Sarah followed Iris' line of sight and turned around, looking where Iris' eyes had frozen. "What?" she said. "Iris!"

The sound of her name brought her back. "Huh? Sorry, wait. Did you see that?"

"See what?" Sarah was concerned.

Iris shook her head. "Nothing... these nightmares. Every night this week. They've become all-consuming. I see this dark figure, I don't know who it is, I can't see a face, but I know it's the person who killed Marie. The littlest sounds make me jump. There're dark shadows around every corner. I can't focus..." Iris' throat tightened with each word she spoke. "Something just feels wrong. I don't know what to do."

Sarah's face softened into concern. "Why don't you

come by my office for a chat? You're going through too much; the stress will bury you alive."

"No. It's not that serious." Iris wiped her face, trying to get rid of any stray tears when she noticed the server walking back to the table.

"Ladies, here we are," he said as he placed their order on the table.

"Oh, yummy. All for me," Sarah said as she rubbed her hands together.

"And I'll take those." Iris pulled the chips close to her. With one elbow on the table and a hand on her forehead, she grabbed the basket and stuffed them, one after the other, into her mouth.

"Jeez, take it easy there." Sarah laughed.

Iris shrugged and kept eating the chips.

AS SARAH FINISHED the last of her pitcher of margaritas, Iris received a call. Sarah made her way over to the bar to chat with a few other patrons while Iris answered her phone, still poking at crumbs that had fallen into the paper-lined chip basket.

"Hi. Where are you?" A sullen voice sounded on the other end of the line.

"Elijah, how are you?" Her face lit up.

"I'm over here at the Cantina. Do you need something?"

"Ugh, I don't know. I guess I just need someone to talk to. Can I crash?"

"Oh sure, come on down." Iris glanced over to the bar. Sarah was trying to climb on top of it with one knee up, but the bartender stopped her.

"Oh, come on, this is my jam. I gotta dance for these

nice men." Sarah's voice filled the small restaurant while the men cheered her on. The bartender shook his head and gestured for her to get down.

"Cool, I'm just down the street. See you in a minute."

"Okay, see you soon." Iris hung up and jumped out of her seat to rush over to Sarah.

"I'm gonna ask you one last time," the bartender was saying as Iris approached them.

"Aw, don't be a buzzkill, man."

"Sorry, sorry, I got her." Iris held up her hands in surrender and pulled on Sarah's arm. "Sarah, come here, come here."

"What?"

"Elijah's coming. You need to chill out. He's gonna be here any minute."

"Oh, my god. He's coming here?" She swayed as she spoke.

"Yes, yes. He's coming here. Are you okay? He wants to talk. Can you control yourself?"

"Pfft!" Sarah flipped her hair back. "Girl, I got this. Don't even worry about me."

ELIJAH WALKED INTO THE BAR. Iris noticed him immediately and got up to greet him at the door.

"Hey." She leaned in for a hug. He embraced her and held her tight. The hug lasted longer than a friendly one. It was the first time the two had seen each other since he'd left, and this time the circumstances were far from familiar.

"Hi, thanks for letting me come by."

"Yeah, yeah, of course. I'm glad you're here. Although, I do think we should have a serious talk, at some point."

Elijah nodded like he knew it was coming.

"Elijah, Elijah..." Sarah called from the bar. "Come, take a shot with me." Iris looked at Elijah, who looked right back at her, ignoring Sarah's call.

"Drink?" Elijah put his hand on the small of her back and led them both to the bar where Sarah was hooting.

Elijah kicked back two rounds. Iris sipped on her water. Sarah galivanted with the other patrons.

"You're not drinking?" Elijah asked.

"Ha, not in her condition." Sarah blurted the words out loud enough for the bartender to hear at the opposite end of the bar.

"Shut up." Iris scowled.

"What?" Elijah looked concerned.

"Nothing. I mean, yeah it's been a long week. I'm too tired to drink."

"Oh please, Iris, you're so full of shit. Tell him about the ba—"

"Hey!" Iris shouted, stopping Sarah from finishing the sentence. Sarah laughed and covered her mouth with her hands.

"Hey?" Elijah took Iris' hand and squeezed it. "Are you okay?"

"Can we go talk? Somewhere private?" Iris glared at Sarah.

"Yeah." Elijah's face looked concerned. "Come on." He hurried them out of the bar and into the parking lot.

"You're acting funny. What's going on?"

"Elijah. I want to be sensitive to you right now, but we do need to talk about what's happening between us. This is the first time I've seen you since..." Iris looked down. She felt her eyes well up as she remembered the pain of receiving his text message. "Why did you leave? Who is she? Why is she better than me?" Iris' voice tensed and became louder with each question.

Elijah bowed his head, locking eyes with the asphalt beneath his feet.

"And now, cause you need someone to talk to, you're reaching out? What about when I needed someone to talk to? You don't even know what's going on with me. You left me alone for two weeks to run your business and clean up your messes. And this woman..." Iris caught herself becoming angry, and took a breath. "I'm sorry. I'm sorry. I don't mean to yell. I know you're going through a lot, but so am I."

"You're not the one who should be apologizing, I. I'm the one." Elijah began to cry as he pressed his fingers against his eyes. "I... I just keep seeing her face. How scared she must have been. How much it must have hurt... I shoulda been there, I shoulda done something... If I wasn't so wrapped up in..." He stopped himself, and instead of finishing the thought, took a deep breath.

"What? Wrapped up in what?"

"Her, the woman, the drinking. I fucked up. Look, look what's happened. To us, to my mom, to everything. It's all fucked up because I'm a fuck up." His shoulders rose and fell as he cried. Tears streamed down his face, and his breath came hard and fast.

"Oh, Elijah..." Watching him in such a state of guilt broke her. She felt her chest constrict, and a ball build up in her throat. She pulled him into a hug. They embraced and cried together. "It's okay. It's okay. None of this is your fault. You can't blame yourself."

"Yes, I. Yes, I can blame myself because this all happened because of me and my bad habit. Now my mom's dead, you're gone, and I have nothing, Ii. Nothing."

"Elijah, you do have something. Or you will..."

Elijah's eyes focused on hers like he was trying to unriddle the puzzle in her words. "What do you mean?"

Faced with confrontation, Iris collapsed into a fit of emotional outpour. "I can't do this..." She choked on words mixed with tears. "It's too much. I can't. I'm sorry."

Without thought, she succumbed to flight and hurried in her walk away from him. He sobbed as she went, increasing in volume and misery with each step she took away from him.

Iris woke in a cold sweat. The bedsheets and her pajamas soaked.

"Marie!" she screamed out loud, pounding her fists on the bed. "I can't do this." Iris grabbed her phone that rested on her bedside table. The glow lit up her face in the otherwise dark room. She scrolled through her contacts until she found Sarah's.

"Hello." A groggy voice answered on the other end.

"Uh... hello? Sarah?" Iris sat up in bed like she was practicing for the role of Regan in The Exorcist. "Sorry, I wasn't expecting you to actually answer."

"I'm here babe, what's up? You okay? You left without saying goodbye."

"I need help." Iris whimpered.

"Oh! Of course. I'm glad you called. You wanna stop by the office? One moment while I pull up my schedule..."

Iris smiled at her friend's formality.

Stillness weighed on both ends of the line. "Um, well, I don't usually work Saturdays, but just come by. I can do it this evening at six o'clock. Cool?"

"Yeah, yeah. That's cool."

"Okay, Iris Callahan at 6 p.m. Got you down."

"Thanks, Doc."

"But, since we're here now, this is quite a troubling hour. Is there something I can help you with right now?"

"Ugh. Don't be so... therapist-y..."

"Well, excuse me, miss thang."

Iris rolled her eyes lightly. "I can't sleep, the nightmares."

"Perfectly reasonable. I understand. Okay, what I want you to do is sit up in bed."

Iris looked around herself. She already was. "Okay."

"Okay, we're gonna take a few deep breaths together, ready?"

Iris listened to her calming breath through the phone. She let herself fall into a rhythm as her breaths trailed in and out of her mouth.

"Okay, good. Now, give your neck a nice little stretch, side to side, up and down."

Silently, Iris followed the direction, listening to the sound of her voice.

"Great job. Are you fully awake now?"

"Yeah, I am."

"Good. Now, we're gonna try a technique called Imagery Rehearsal Therapy, okay? Just for a moment, while I have you on the phone."

"Okay."

"You're going to keep your eyes open and be present in your safe space. You're safe here in your bedroom, okay? And I want you to imagine the last scary thing you dreamed of but don't worry, listen to my voice. I'm here with you, and you're safe. When you're ready, tell me what you see."

"Uh... I see a shadowy man... I can't see his face; he's

more of a presence." Iris gulped, her breathing becoming shallow.

"It's okay, Iris. I'm right here with you. Try to slow down and take deeper breaths."

"Okay. He's standing behind her... Her face is full of blood..."

"Okay, okay, now, Iris, stay with me. Now we're going to imagine there's no blood. Okay, you're in charge here. We're going to change the scene. No blood, no darkness, and give him a face. Can you do that? Take another deep breath and tell me what you see now."

"Okay." Iris took a breath. Her voice calmed as she repainted the picture in her mind. "Her face is clean. It's daytime. The man is stepping forward. It's... Elijah?"

"Great, great job. Now, Elijah is just a man, nothing scary about him, right?"

"Yes. But why him? This isn't right." Anxiety tightened her voice.

"It's okay. It's all okay. This is typical when we reimagine our trauma. We replace the negative images with comforting ones. This is just your mind's way of rectifying a terrifying experience with something calming. Sometimes it appears a bit confusing, but we're gonna work on that, okay?"

"Okay." The explanation was enough to compose Iris. She slumped back into her pillows.

"Now, if you have these nightmares again, I want you to remember that you are in control, you are safe, and you can change the picture. Okay? You wake yourself up completely and reimagine the scene. Don't let the dark presence win. Change it into whatever else you want it to be."

"Okay, I'll try."

"Great. We will go deeper into this at the office, but for

now, keep breathing and see if it doesn't at least help you get a little more sleep this morning, okay?"

"Thanks, Sarah."

"No problem, now leave me alone." Iris laughed again at Sarah's change in personality.

By the time Iris clicked off, she was no longer scared but still confused. Had she imagined Elijah's face only because the sight of him was calming? The narrative made sense, but it didn't at the same time. At least, in this version of her visions, Marie was no longer bloody or dead. She was alive, and Elijah was Elijah. To see the two of them together wasn't anything unusual. It probably meant nothing. She wrote it off as a trick her subconscious had conjured to imagine something different.

It was 3:45 a.m. There was still plenty of time to sleep. As she drifted off, Elijah's face popped in and out, but her nightmarish visions stayed away. For the first time in too long, she rested well.

TWENTY-SIX

The day wouldn't end fast enough. As it wore on, Iris became distressed. The few hours of sleep she'd gotten in the morning hadn't afforded her enough energy to last the entire day, and her visions returned. The trick of imagining something less scary wasn't working in the eerie office hallways and dark corners of the studio.

Iris stood behind the furnace and loaded it with coals for the evening class. The studio was empty, and the only light source came from an early evening sun that chased the shadows out through the open warehouse doors lining the back wall. The instructor for the evening was a local glass artist named Adam, but he hadn't arrived yet, and the rest of the staff had gone home. Iris took it upon herself to ready the class and prep the stations before his arrival so she'd be able to leave and have enough time to make it across town to meet at Sarah's office.

The fire burned only inches from her face, making her brow sweat. She felt a presence approach from behind.

"Adam is that—" She turned to greet the instructor but stopped short when she realized no one there. A tingle crept down her spine. Frightened, she turned back toward the furnace to finish her task and leave the space that now felt unsafe. She poked the coals again, more quickly this time.

The crash of a glass vase falling to the floor made her jolt her head toward the noise. She gasped and froze like a deer caught in the bright shine of oncoming headlights. Her sight rummaged through the open space, looking for the source of the sound, pieces of glass, or movement, but found nothing out of place. Nothing broken.

She shivered and turned back toward the furnace, only this time standing in front of her was the dark, faceless figure. She screamed, jumped, and fell backward, crashing into a side table of tools and glass working utensils. By the time she'd gathered herself back up off the floor, it had vanished. She peered at the nooks and crannies her eyeline could reach from where she stood. Again, there was nothing. She waited, keeping herself so still only the sound of her beating heart vibrated through the space. When she felt sure that it had left for good, she yelled in frustration. She gathered herself in a huddle and hugged her shoulders, a meager attempt at self-comfort.

"Iris?" A man's voice came from beyond the open warehouse doors.

"Adam? Hi." Iris laughed and shook herself, releasing her clenched muscles. "Oh gosh, sorry about that, I just tripped and had a little moment. Sorry."

"No worries, you sure you're okay?"

"Yeah, yeah, thanks…" Avoiding eye contact, she set to work picking up the instruments she'd knocked over in the fall. "Um, I finished setting up for tonight. Your class should arrive any minute. You need anything else before I take off?"

"Nope, all good. Oh, is Elijah here?"

"No, he's not in tonight. Can you lock up after you're done?"

"Sure thing."

Iris hurried back to her office to grab her things and fix her face. Approaching each corner with apprehension, she peeked around first to inspect the area and avoid any more surprises.

TWENTY-SEVEN

Sarah's office building was a converted Painted Lady, an old Victorian house in pastel purples, greens, and gold trimmings. A lobby and reception area were made up in the converted sitting room. The decor was representative of the time the home was built, but the extra chairs, old magazines, and motivational posters on the walls screamed clinical establishment.

No one greeted her at reception. The only indication of her presence was the bell hanging from the door, triggered as she entered. Within the minute, Sarah came from a hallway and presented herself.

"You made it," Sarah said. The meeting was awkward. Never had the two met under such formal circumstances. Iris had never even been inside Sarah's office. She wore a black blazer and a pencil skirt. The professional clothing Iris was accustomed to, but in this context, it was different, coupled with an attitude of a professional woman and sans a margarita. This was a different Sarah, and it took Iris almost by surprise.

"Hi. This is weird. You look weird. Is this weird?" Iris

questioned herself for even considering using her best friend as her hired therapist.

"It's not weird. This is my job, and I'm glad you're here." Sarah motioned for Iris to follow and led her back through the hall and into an office that was once a bedroom. It felt typical of any therapy office she'd ever seen on television or read in a book with a long velvet sofa, much like the very one Iris had in her living room, only this was mustard yellow as opposed to her own hunter green. The yellow had been her second choice. A coffee table and an armchair completed the set, the colors coordinated and finished in a mid-century modern feel that deviated from the Victorian decor of the reception area.

A box of tissues lay on the coffee table. Another box rested on an end table that sat at the right end of the sofa's arm, and a third on the opposite end at the corner of the room. A large area rug covered most of the hardwood floor and a large wall clock rested on the wall above the sofa, visible only to whoever was sitting in the adjacent armchair.

"Please, have a seat." Sarah gestured to the velvet sofa.

"Okay, you're really gonna have to stop doing that. The therapist talk is freaking me out."

Sarah giggled. "Well, you are here for therapy, aren't you?" She smiled and maintained eye contact as she spoke.

Iris shrugged and sunk down into her seat while crossing her arms over her chest.

"I think it'll be easier for us to go through some of the exercises if I maintain a therapeutic style of speaking. I want you to feel comfortable talking to me, but this is not casual, this is work, so it will feel different, but you'll get used to it. Sound good?"

Iris nodded. "Yeah, I guess."

"Okay, so, Iris, I'll save you the trouble of rehashing for

me exactly what's going on with you since I know the history. But let's start with how you're feeling right now."

"Um, okay..." Iris thought for a moment, not knowing where to start. "I guess I've been under a lot of stress. The nightmares have become visions. And it all stems from him, I can't stop thinking about it... If that makes sense?"

"That makes perfect sense. Can you define who he is to you, without using his name, we both know I already know it." Sarah chuckled.

"Well, I guess it's kinda complicated, right? He's my ex-fiancé, my boss, first love, and father of my unborn child... Yeah, that about sums it up."

"First love, you say. Can you elaborate on that?"

Iris became uncomfortable like she'd said something she shouldn't have. She wasn't ready to have that conversation. "Um." Iris shook her head. "No, I just mean... well I've known him forever, so when we finally got together, we fell fast for each other. I didn't mean I loved him before..." Iris mumbled to herself. "Stupid..."

"Why is it stupid?"

Iris shook her head again, stronger this time, dying to change the subject. "Anyway, I'm terrified to go to sleep at night." Iris paused to chew on a thought. "How do I make the nightmares go away?" Iris slumped in her seat, her eyes welling up.

Sarah pushed over the box of tissues. "Does he know about the pregnancy, yet?"

"No, I still haven't told him." Iris patted the tissue under her eyes to catch the tears as they fell.

"Okay. I ask because I think a big part of why you're having nightmares, and now visions are because you're holding onto this. Why do you think it's important for you to keep the pregnancy a secret?"

Iris was puzzled. "I mean, I'm not doing it intentionally, it just hasn't been a good time."

"Do you feel like maybe you have had opportunities to tell him, but you're not because you're putting his feelings and trauma before your own?"

"I already told you." Iris' tone was sharp. "It wouldn't be right, not right now, with everything he's going through."

"That's understandable, but only to a degree. Perhaps it wasn't appropriate when he first told you about his mother, but it's been a couple of weeks, and he's since reached out to you. Now would be a good time. The two of you can take this opportunity to heal together."

"I'd always hoped we'd have a family someday, but not like this. I don't want him coming back out of obligation because I got knocked up. And I don't know what's going on with this other woman or if she's still in the picture."

"That must be incredibly hard for you."

"Yes, I mean, everything about this feels tragic, like some crazy daytime soap opera, but you can't make this stuff up." Iris shook her head and scoffed.

"Okay, the nightmares and visions. I want you to keep practicing the technique I showed you. Don't expect them to disappear overnight, but as we keep working here and deal with some of the issues, and you do the work, they'll become less tormenting, and eventually, we're gonna get through it all. Both of us, together. Okay?"

"Okay."

"Now, it's clear you're still feeling uncomfortable about the pregnancy and how you want to disclose that to Elijah."

Iris nodded.

"So, why don't you hold off on that for now. We have some time and this is your decision and it's a big one, so you need to be ready. We'll keep working on it, and my goal is to get you to the place where you feel confident about it. Okay?"

"I feel good about that. Thanks."

"Of course. Like your mom said, always here for anything you need."

Iris chuckled. "Great... Wait, are we still friends? Can I call you later or?"

Sarah scoffed and rolled her eyes, removing her metaphorical therapist's hat. "Oh, my god, yes, stupid!"

Iris smiled in relief recognizing her friend and waved before walking away. It was dark outside, but inside she felt lighter and uplifted. She looked forward to that evening, confident that it would be free of nightmares.

Iris slept well that night and woke up on Sunday morning feeling renewed and ready to apologize to Elijah for how she'd left him in the parking lot.

"Hello?" Elijah answered.

"Hey. How are you?"

Elijah didn't respond, but Iris imagined him shrugging.

"Sorry, I know, stupid question... Anyway, I wanted to call and check in. It's Sunday. I thought maybe we could have brunch. Like we used to? I can come cook for you if you're up for it?"

"Where is this coming from?" Elijah's voice was stern and accusatory.

"I know. I'm sorry. I'm so sorry. It was selfish of me to leave you like that, and there's no excuse. I know you're the one hurting right now, and I want to help you."

"You're the only one who can, Ii. You. Just you. I'm alone in this world now."

"I'm so sorry, Elijah. But you're not alone. I'm still here." The line went silent as Iris paused. "Listen, let me come cook for you. Okay?"

Elijah let out a sigh. "Yeah, okay."

"Okay, great. Um, where are you?"

"I'm at my mom's since it... happened." Elijah took his time getting out the words.

Her chest sank as she gulped the ball stuck in her throat. Marie lived in the

not-so-savory part of downtown. Yes, it was a house, but could have been mistaken for a condemned teardown if someone added the minor feature of boarded windows to the front. Marie's parents gifted the house to her before they passed. Through years of neglect and abuse, it all but fell apart. Elijah made promises to fix it up for her, to make it more livable. Instead, he spent his parental visitation hours with June, fulfilling his 'son duties' there.

"Okay, I'll be there soon." Iris shivered, realizing she'd agreed to go visit him at a dead woman's home.

THE HOUSE LOOKED DIFFERENT—DARKER like someone had scrubbed a gray hue of dirty dishwater into the paint. The gate was broken and creaky; the boards looked more cracked—overall more disjointed than she remembered.

Elijah greeted her at the screen door that squealed to open and close. "Hey, come in." His eyes were downcast as she entered the house in shambles. Clothes were strewn about on the floor, and there were empty food containers and dog feces everywhere. Two little barking Ballpark Dogs came running from the back hallway to meet her. They skittered around her ankles and wagged their tails. Iris called them Ballpark Dogs because it was easier to say than Dachshund. Elijah chuckled at her every time she tried and mispronounced it. Ballpark, she could say, and because he liked baseball, he laughed at the reference.

"Mini! Tiny! Hi, my babies!" Iris greeted them and picked them up. "Has daddy been taking care of you? Hi, yes, hello..."

Elijah smiled. His mother's dogs were the only thing he had left of her.

"Thanks for coming. Looks like the pups missed you."

"Oh, of course. I'm happy to come by and see these little loves anytime." She gave them each one last kiss and sat them back down on the ground. "Now, food first, or should I help you clean up a bit?"

Elijah shrugged.

"Why don't I just clean up a bit? Won't take long. And then we'll get started on your waffles."

"Thanks." Elijah plopped himself down on the couch and huddled up as Iris reached down to gather fallen clothing. She couldn't leave the space like this. *A clean space is a clean mind*, her mother always told her, and she lived by those words.

Iris moved her way through the living room, kitchen, bedrooms, and bathrooms, cleaning up the messes as she went. She started breakfast after putting in a load of laundry. Elijah stayed on the couch with his phone while the dogs played with their toys in the now clean living room.

"Okay." Iris came from the kitchen with two hot plates of banana waffles, sausages, and poached eggs. She presented one to Elijah, who sat up straight and smiled at her.

"This looks great, Ii. Thanks."

"Your favorites!"

The dogs begged and jumped around their shins and

barked for scraps. Elijah threw them little bits while Iris laughed.

"I really appreciate you doing this. Thank you," said Elijah as he looked into Iris' eyes and placed his hand on her thigh.

"Oh... I did this for five years; it's no different now."

"That's exactly what I mean. You've taken care of me for so long, and I never appreciated you. Thank you, for all of that, and I'm sorry for not saying it more often."

Iris felt her chest tighten as she soaked up the sincerity in Elijah's face. She wanted to speak, but the words refused to come.

"I know there were a lot of things I didn't do right in our relationship, and I see now what it's cost me. You being here now proves to me I screwed up the best thing I ever had."

"Oh, Elijah..." Tears fell from her eyes in a single steady stream.

"I love you, Ii. Now more than ever. I've been so stupid." He leaned in to kiss her, and she let their lips touch.

The static from the touch built up an electric flow inside her chest as dopamine surged through her brain. She took deep breaths as he groped at her skin and pulled her into him, the plates nearly crashing.

"Stop!" She pulled away, a hand on his chest while she pushed him back, a half-eaten plate of banana waffles still on her lap. "We can't do this. I'm sorry."

Elijah put his head into his hands and ran his fingers through his short hair. "I'm sorry. I'm sorry. I don't know what I was thinking."

"No, no. It's fine, it's just..." But she couldn't say the words as she watched him succumb into himself and turn into a blubbering mess of a lost little boy.

"I just can't believe she's gone. I couldn't save her." The words wrestled their way out. The conversation wasn't about them anymore. She adopted a more supportive stance and comforted him while she rubbed his back.

"Elijah, there was nothing anyone could have done to save her." She didn't know what else to say. She searched for the right words, but her mind came up blank. It didn't seem to matter though, as he hugged her and held onto her. The ex-lovers embraced, and she let his tears stain her clothing. Her heart hurt for him. She gathered her strength and used it against the weight of his body, holding him up, physically and otherwise.

"You know." Elijah took a breath and calmed himself enough to let words out freely. "She really loved you. She always told me that you would be the perfect woman to settle down with and have a family."

The word struck a chord through her, and her shoulders crumbled. A seething burn crept into her chest as she gasped for air. Her eyes watered and overcame her. She wanted more than anything to spit out the words—all was not lost; they could be a family. He wasn't alone and would never be alone again. She could do that for him; she could save him. But the tension in her chest kept her throat from opening. It became so tight that the air she drew in could no longer fill her lungs. She couldn't breathe.

Sadness switched to panic as she coughed and gasped for air, her eyes wide and face red.

"Ii? Are you okay? What can I do?"

Iris shook her head, unable to speak. She stood and paced the living room, coughing for air as the walls closed in. The dark presence filled the room and concentrated around her. The space became smaller, smaller still.

"I can't breathe!" It was like something had sucked the oxygen out of the house and the world.

A voice from nowhere materialized into the darkness. *"Run"*.

TWENTY-NINE

Her legs carried her out of the house and into her car where she caught her breath. Several deep inhales reduced the burning in her lungs as she relished in the fresh air.

The release was fleeting because the panic followed her. Elijah's voice called out for her, but she couldn't see him anywhere. The road was in front of her, surrounded by darkness that faded into nothing. Tunnel vision. The only other item she could see was her cell phone. Her breath quickened as her trembling fingers pecked at the screen, searching for Sarah's contact number. She found it and dialed.

"Hey, what's up?"

"Sarah…" Iris breathed heavily and deeply as she hyper-ventilated into the microphone.

"Yes, I'm here, Iris. How can I help you?" Therapist Sarah responded.

"I… Uh…"

"It's okay, listen to my voice." Sarah slowed down and breathed deeply over the line. The sound of her breathing calmed Iris until the two were breathing together, slow and deep. Inhale, exhale. "Keep breathing... a few more. Inhale, exhale... Now, when you're ready, why don't you tell me what's going on?"

"Okay..." Inhale, exhale. "I don't know... I was just at Elijah's, and it happened. The darkness." Her consciousness slowly returned as her vision sharpened. The scene shifted from total blackness to a glum gray.

"Iris, considering the immense amount of stress you're under, you're bound to have physical symptoms."

"Yeah, but this was different. It was dark, so dark." Iris' breath quickened again, and her voice adopted a higher pitch.

"Take a breath. It's okay. Iris, there is a range of experiences one might endure while under stress. These include visual and auditory hallucinations, disassociations, paranoia, and of course, physical symptoms like tightening in the chest and throat, hot flashes, increased heart rate, cold sweats. I'm sure that everything you've just experienced can be explained with logic."

"Okay, you're right. Yeah, you're right."

"What were you and Elijah talking about when this occurred?"

"About his mother. And he said that she had always wanted him and I to settle down and have a family, a baby."

"I see. How did that make you feel?"

"We are having a baby, and I can't tell him. He's all alone now, and I could save him from that. He doesn't have to be alone anymore." Iris felt herself becoming overwhelmed again. She banged her head onto her steering wheel and sobbed, grappling with her thoughts.

"Being alone is a big fear of yours, Iris."

"I mean... so?" she said, distracted away from further self-harm.

"Okay, try to separate yourself from him. You don't want to project your own feelings onto him right now. Remember, he's going through something extremely traumatic, same as you, but they are two very different things."

"Yeah..." Iris sighed. "But what if it helps? It could be the answer that he's been searching for—a relief from the nightmare."

"Iris, babies should be brought into happy environments. They do not create happiness just by their existence. Do you agree?"

She sighed again. "I guess."

"We already discussed how being rash about this is not the right way. There will be a right time for you to share this news, but out of fear is not it. Remember what we talked about? Confidence. First, we need to build back your confidence."

The panic released its hold on her. A brightness came into the sky, and she wiped stale tears away from her face.

"So, what do I do now? I'm still here, outside his house."

"Where is he? Is he waiting for you? Looking for you?"

Iris paused and looked toward the front door. "No. He's not."

"Okay, that's fine. He probably needs some time right now. If I were you, I would text him and apologize for running out. Tell him you're fine but going to go home and rest."

"But what if he needs me?"

"He needs a lot more than what you can give him right now. You have to first take care of yourself before you can take care of anyone else. This is a process."

"Wow, you're like, really good at your job." Iris chuckled. "It's like you're in my head."

Sarah laughed. "Just trying to help."

Iris woke up on Monday morning feeling refreshed and rejuvenated. The knowledge that life was growing inside her brought a serenity as she pushed away the negative thoughts that hovered from the day before. She brushed powder on her face and thought about Elijah, wondering if he would be back at the studio today. She missed seeing him around and wanted to return to some degree of normalcy.

The sunshine was extra bright that day as she drove to the studio. A blue sky with puffy, happy clouds allowed the sun's glow to shower down on her. She drove with her window down so she could listen to the birds' chirping and song. At stoplights, she smiled as they fluttered and danced in the sky. She rubbed her belly and described to her unborn child the beautiful morning scenery.

"HAPPY MONDAY!" Jessica greeted. "How are you today?"

"Hi," Iris said. "You're chipper this morning."

"Oh, well of course I am. It's a beautiful day."

"Okay..." Iris kept walking, shaking her head.

"Have a wonderful day!" Jessica shouted at Iris' back, waving her arms, unable to contain her excitement.

<hr>

THE DAY MOVED QUICKLY. It was time for lunch. The morning had been full of interruptions by office staff and studio artists, who all wanted to come to say hello, or offer their condolences for Elijah's mother. By now the news of what happened had begun to spread and Iris fielded questions and concerns, not about glass blowing, but about Elijah, how he was doing, and the police investigation.

She figured it was probably best that he wasn't at work. Better she is the one they directed the questions to than a broken man not strong enough to face the emotional consequences.

"Hey, Iris. How the heck are ya?" Eric, a local artist, came to her office. He was a greasy, long-haired hippie type who smoked pot outside the warehouse and wore the same t-shirt and jeans with burn holes every day. He was also a friend of Marie's, Iris figured she'd be seeing him soon and expected to have to console him.

"Hey, Eric. I'm good. How are you?"

"I am doing just excellent. I wanted to come say hi. Happy Monday!"

"Yeah." Iris chuckled, the Beaver Cleaver aura that surrounded the day continuing through.

"Great, yeah... Heard about Marie. Such a shame."

"Oh, thank you. Yeah, it's very sad. Elijah's dealing with it."

"Thank goodness, that is such a relief. He's so lucky to have someone like you looking out for him and the studio."

"You seem in high spirits today? You and everyone, actually."

"Oh yeah, you know..." Eric bobbed his head in agreement, but offered no further explanation. "Well, anyway. Nice talking to ya. You let us know what you end up finding out or if there's anything any of us can do?"

"Yeah, sure, Eric. Thanks."

"Alright!" Still standing in the doorway, Eric flashed a grin and slapped the frame a couple of times before walking back to the studio.

Iris shook her head and rolled her eyes. "What the heck is in the water today?"

IRIS RECEIVED a text message from Elijah.

The police are here, please come. They're gonna take me!

Iris gasped and sprang into action.

I'm on my way! She replied and grabbed her things, shouting to Jessica as she hurried out the door. "Jessica, can you lock up tonight?"

"No problem, everything okay?"

"Yeah, gotta go. Thanks!"

Her heart raced as her legs directed her body out to her car. Her thoughts weighed heavily on her mind, matching the weight of her foot on the gas pedal. Were the police arresting him? Did they think he did it? Not knowing what to think, her thoughts only took her down a rabbit hole that led to a cascading wave of anxiety and endless questions.

She arrived outside Marie's home. A police car was pulling out. The car ride had left her feeling unsure about who she might encounter when she arrived. A police offi-cer? Elijah in handcuffs? An empty house? The man had a troubled soul but wasn't murderous. The back and forth brought her nowhere closer to a conclusion. He would be the only one to give her answers. Assured, but still nervous, she parked and took the steps toward the front door, half expecting Elijah wouldn't answer.

THIRTY-ONE

The muffled sound of the doorbell vibrated through the other side. She shivered at the fall of fast and heavy footsteps responding to the bell.

"Ii! Oh, my god, Ii. Thank god," Elijah said as he opened the door, deflated and downcast. He was a ruined man standing before her. Anxiety washed out of her veins and replaced itself with an overwhelming need to mother him. She reached out and cradled his head as he collapsed into her arms. His sobs pulled him heavier into her with each breath, in and out. The rise and fall of his chest on hers cemented their bodies closer together. Still standing in the doorway, she held him for several minutes before speaking and soaked in the euphoric dopamine rush that flowed through her, his need for her bringing it to life.

"Elijah, what's wrong?"

He tried to speak, but his whimpering stopped him. His puffy eyes and tear-stained cheeks spoke to her where words failed.

"It's okay, it's okay. Come on. Let's sit down." She led Elijah into the house, settling on the couch with her hand resting on his thigh. "Let's take a few deep breaths, okay?" She ran him through the exercises that Sarah had practiced with her.

After several breaths, Elijah had quieted enough to speak. "They think I did it. They think I killed her."

"Not possible. They didn't arrest you. They're not charging you. How could they think that?"

"They told me to stay in town. That they might need more information from me."

"Okay, that sounds pretty standard, right? You were the closest person to her and it makes sense that they would want to stay in contact with you until they have a suspect."

Elijah stared blankly at Iris. The moment became uncomfortable. Iris wiggled in her seat and pulled at her blouse.

"Tell me what happened… when the police showed up? What did they ask? What did you say?"

Elijah sighed and leaned back on the couch, lifting his arms and resting them behind his head in a relaxed and open position. His eyes focused on a spot on the ceiling.

"They told me they were coming. I thought they were gonna tell me they found the guy, that they knew what happened to her and this whole thing was gonna be over. But then they started asking questions. The detective, in the suit, asked me the regular CSI bullshit stuff. Where was I the night it happened, what I was doing, who I was with… I told him I was with…" Elijah paused. Iris tensed and closed her eyes, bracing herself for what was coming next.

"It's okay, you can say it."

"Well, I told them I was with… her. They asked if she could verify that. But I also came here, to mom's house, found her with some dude. I told them she asked me for money, I said no, and she left. I followed them down to The Tenderloin."

"Wait, wait…" Iris held up her hands and shook her head, trying to understand. "Did you go down there… with her?" Iris was no longer talking about Marie but the woman he'd left her for.

"No, no. It wasn't like that. I had to see her after though, I'd been staying with her since I left… you… anyway." Elijah shook his head. "I lost them and couldn't find my mom anywhere."

Iris felt her heart harden in her chest. She didn't like being reminded of the other woman, but it was part of the reality now. At least he was being honest with her and he was sparing her the gory details of their intimate encounters.

"But why didn't you tell me you went down looking for her?"

"Because I forgot. I went down again the next day when I still hadn't heard from her. I jumbled up the dates."

Iris nodded while the lump in her throat grew like a tumor, fed with each heavy beat of her heart.

"I told the detective that I saw some people she hangs out with. That they were acting shifty and wouldn't look me in the eye or answer my questions. So, I followed one of them. Down an alley and stayed back while I watched him cop from his dealer. I heard them talking. And he said it, Ii. He said it."

"Said what?" Iris' eyes widened.

"He said that Marie finally got her head bashed in. That she was in a tent and they were looking for a couple of guys to help move her body. They were gonna move it to a dumpster behind the Chinese restaurant. Something about how the place had the rankest trash and she wouldn't be found for a while."

"What?" Iris yelled as the shock swept through her. "Why didn't you tell that to the cops the first time?" Iris felt blood heat in her body, her breathing becoming heavy as she compensated for the lack of oxygen that seemed to burn out of the room.

Elijah looked at her, he didn't have a response, only a look of confusion on his wide-eyed face. Iris's chest sunk with the gravity of his confession. The darkness crept in to overcome the space.

"I didn't know..."

The light sucked out of the room, and she spiraled into her nightmares. She was outside. The night made the hairs on her body stand on end and her breath billow in a cloud of steam from her mouth. She saw Marie, blood pouring down her face as she whimpered toward a shadowy figure, begging, pleading for her life. The shadow lifted as she recognized the face. The sound of shattering glass shook the sky as she watched Marie fall to the ground before Elijah's feet.

Iris let out a blood-curdling scream that brought her back to the living room. The sight of Elijah next to her shook her bones. "It was you!"

"No! Ii..." Elijah leaned forward with arms stretched out toward her.

"Get away from me!" Iris screamed and ran from him. The weight of her oxygen-deprived body dragged her down and slowed her movements. She fought to reach the door outside where she knew a breath of air was waiting for her.

THIRTY-TWO

"Ii!" She heard Elijah scream. Her legs sprung with energy and carried her away from him. In the safety of her car, she heaved and panted. High-pitched sounds escaped her throat as her chest rose and fell. Her face tingled with blood pumping through her skin. Without thinking, she drove, not knowing where she was going or what she would do next; her only goal was to get as far away from the man she now realized was a murderer.

When the unknown road stretched out in front of her brought her no more relief, she picked up her phone with a shaky hand. Sweat smeared across the touchscreen as she thumbed through her contacts until she landed on Sarah's name.

"Sup." Her voice was a welcome reprieve, but still not enough to bring Iris' breathing to relax.

"Sarah. Oh, my god, Sarah. It... it's him. He—her!"

"Iris, calm down. Take a breath... I'm here, it's okay. Breathe with me, please."

"Breathe? Oh, my god. No! I feel like I'm stuck in some fucking time loop. Every time I come over here, this happens! I can't... I..." Iris hyperventilated as she choked through her words. She hurdled forward into a complete meltdown.

"Iris, I'm here for you. Please listen to my voice. Take a deep breath in..."

Before she knew it, and without trying to, Iris was breathing in time with Sarah while tears streamed down her cheeks and her face flushed.

"Good, good. Now, tell me what happened."

"It was him, Sarah. It was Elijah. He killed her." Iris broke down again.

"Iris, where are you now?"

Iris snapped back into her surroundings and looked for a street sign or some landmark that would answer the question. "I'm downtown by the Cantina."

"You're very close to my office. I'm here now. Why don't you come in?"

"Okay, okay, I'll be there."

THE SIGHT of Sarah waiting for her in the lobby brought the broken sobbing back. Overwhelmed by the weight of what she was going through, Iris let tears fall from her eyes and wailed.

Sat in Sarah's office, "why don't you walk me through exactly what happened at Elijah's?"

"I went there because he was upset." Iris spoke through her tears, but her breathing remained aggravated. "He told me... that he heard them talking. He knew how it happened and when, but he never told the police. How could he know and not say anything? He's guilty!" She was getting hysterical. Unable to stay seated any longer, she paced back and forth along the length of the couch.

"Iris, Iris..." Sarah lowered her voice further and spoke slower, almost in a whisper. "Before we go any further, let's think about this. Did Elijah give this information to the police?"

"Eventually."

"And they didn't arrest him?"

"Well, no..."

"Okay, then that's a pretty good sign that he hasn't done anything suspicious enough for them to think he's a suspect, right?"

Iris stayed silent.

"We don't need to panic. I'd like to try something with you if you're open to it?"

Iris nodded, but she didn't stop pacing. She brought a shaking hand to the edge of her teeth and bit at her nails.

"I'd like to try hypnosis. To calm you and help you gather your thoughts."

Hypnosis! The idea froze her like she was encased in stone.

"Something wrong?"

"Hypnosis... isn't that where you could like make me quack like a duck or steal all my money?" Iris imagined herself theatrically acting out such suggestions and what a fool it would make of her. A flash of a memory came to her; she had seen it happen on The Maury Show when she was a kid.

Sarah laughed. "Not at all. This isn't daytime television. I could never do such a thing. Hypnosis is a legitimate technique that allows me to help you release anxiety and tension. While it is true you are more inclined to suggestions under this state, you do not lose complete control over your own will and behavior."

"Um, okay."

"Please sit down and make yourself comfortable."

Iris hesitated but agreed. Her knee jolted up and down as she tapped her foot on the carpet. Sarah held a soft hand over Iris' knee to calm it, but it only led to tapping her fingers on the couch.

"Okay, Iris. I need you to take a deep breath for me... Again, please. I'm breathing with you." The two of them repeated the process, in and out.

THIRTY-THREE

In a deep hypnotic state, Iris floated through the memory of her reconnection with Elijah that fateful day she'd walked into his studio for an interview. The meeting. The date. The dinner. The magic. Sarah's voice took her through the experience again like it was happening for the first time.

"Tell me where you are now, what you're doing? Describe the scene, please?" Sarah's quiet voice hardly intruded but acted as a gentle reminder for Iris to speak.

"We're in Golden Gate Park with Ma. She made a picnic for us. I can see the bridge." A smile came to Iris' face. "There's a field overhung by trees. Ma has a checkered blanket out. Wine. Snacks." Iris giggled. "She likes him. He's being so sweet too, who wouldn't?" The replay calmed her as she relaxed into the crevices of a time when she was falling in love.

June truly loved Elijah in the beginning. Iris gushed to her about how romantic he was, how attentive he was, how special he made her feel. She talked about his past. Though he was born out of hardship and had watched a man overdose in a crack house with his father at the age of five, he didn't let his circumstances define him. Elijah was a good man that needed love. It was love that Iris had to give, and her mother showered it upon him too when she welcomed him into their little family of two.

"Good, good. What's happening now?"

Iris' face tensed like she could sense danger but couldn't yet see it. "Oh... wait..." Her face relaxed. "My birthday party. The one you threw for me. I'm meeting him for the first time. He's so tall, so handsome. Those silly snake bite piercings on his lips." Iris disappeared into the fantasy. She recalled how Elijah had flirted with her, how she felt swept up in him. "But..." Confusion took her again. "He's gone. It's dark. The water is cold. What's happening?" Iris panicked, not understanding where these memories were coming from. She opened her eyes to find her naked body in a dark bathroom, the cold sting of a running shower hitting her skin. Afraid and alone, she huddled into a fetal position and rocked herself back and forth. "Where am I? What's happening? Sarah!" Iris screamed at the top of her lungs, driven by pure terror.

"Take me somewhere else. What was the first year of your relationship like?" Sarah said the words, snapped her fingers together, and Iris was back to Elijah, back to a more difficult but familiar point in their relationship. It was a time when Elijah was staying out late, drinking, picking fights with Iris for reasons she could only assume became his justifications for not coming home.

Iris woke up at six in the morning to his side of the bed still cold, and no sign of him in the apartment. She called him a dozen times, each time the phone rang until the voicemail picked up. This was somehow reassuring to her because it meant he wasn't in jail. She knew the first thing police officers did when taking in a suspect under arrest was turn off their phones. A tidbit of information she picked up after the first time Elijah was arrested for drunk driving.

When she couldn't get a hold of him on his phone, she began calling the nearby hospitals. None of them had patients by his name, no unidentified emergency room John Doe's to speak of. The last call, to her mother, solidified her growing suspicion that he was up to no good. The memory took her right back to the phone call.

"Mom?" Iris heard her voice tremble as she laid back on Sarah's couch, deep in a hypnotic state.

"Hi, sweetheart. It's so early. Everything okay?"

"Elijah. The hospital. He's nowhere." Iris' voice came out in a staccato. "I don't know what to do!"

"Slow down, baby. I can't understand you. What are you trying to say?"

Her breathing quickened as she dove deeper.

"Iris..." The sound of Sarah's voice distracted her. "I don't want you to focus on your negative memories. Take me back to the picnic in the park with Elijah and your mom. Wasn't that a nice moment?"

"These aren't memories... It's something different."

"Let's move on. What's happening at the picnic?"

Her visions switched back quickly to the serenity of the park, like a television flipping between channels.

Iris sipped on wine and ate cheese as she looked off into the fog-filled sky, marveling at the orange bridge that towered over them.

"Elijah. What's this new piece you're working on? The fire heart vase, I think Iris called it?" June was always good at making people feel comfortable. Always let them talk about themselves, her mother always told her.

"Oh, yeah. It's something I've been wanting to do for a while. It's a vase with a glass heart inside, and the facets of the glass make it look like it's burning, on fire. It's a combination of glass blowing and carving to make the facets." Elijah puffed out his chest.

"Good," said Sarah's ethereal voice as if it were coming through the fog. "What happens next?"

"You know, we just landed a new account at the studio. A glassware company hired Elijah to custom-make a special line of designer vases. This is the first piece in the collection."

"If I can pull it off." Elijah chuckled at himself.

"Oh, my! How exciting! How did you pull that off?"

"Yeah, thank you. It is exciting. Iris has really helped a lot with the logistics since coming to work for me. If it wasn't for her, I never would have put myself out there and gone after that account."

"Well, my girl is very special. You probably don't even deserve to be with her. The son of a drug-addicted whore and a pimp? Serves your mother right, she went and got herself killed."

"What? No. That's not what she said." Iris shook her head in confusion. "This isn't how it happened..." The sky turned black. The park disappeared, along with the checkered blanket, the wine and cheese, and the bridge. Left standing in the darkness were only Iris, June, and Elijah.

"It was you, wasn't it? You not only knocked up my daughter, you killed your poor mother!" Iris' mother advanced at Elijah with a finger sticking out in front of her face, aimed for his throat. The sound of shattering glass followed and pulled Iris out of the darkness.

Her eyes widened and she let out a frightened yelp as she came back to her body and into Sarah's office.

"It's okay, Iris. You're okay. You're safe here with me."

"What happened?" She grabbed her chest and saw

blood on her knuckles when she looked down. "Why am I bleeding?" Iris screamed the words and stood up, searching the room for answers. "Did you do this to me? Did you make me do this to myself?" Her muscles tensed and her heart sent adrenaline pumping through her body.

"Iris. I need you to calm down." Sarah's voice remained low and slow. She held out her hands in a gesture of surrender, urging Iris to calm herself. "It's okay. We had an accident, and you knocked over a picture frame. It must have cut your hand when you hit it."

"Bullshit. You did this!" Her pupils were so wide the color disappeared from them. Her face flushed red, and her legs tingled, forcing her to move. Standing up, she paced the room and felt a crunch beneath her feet. She looked down. Pieces of glass littered the floor, and a broken frame lay face down from where it fell.

"Careful of the glass, please." Sarah reached for a box of tissues. "Please, take these and wipe your hand. It's okay. You're safe here, Iris. I'm here to help."

Iris took a moment to process the hallucination, the reality, and how the two connected. Unable to make sense of it, or not wanting to, she ignored Sarah's offer and clutched her stomach.

"I feel sick. I have to go." With no further explanation and not giving Sarah a chance to stop her, she left the office and ran out the front door and into the familiar security of her getaway car.

THIRTY-FOUR

Iris slammed the front door of her apartment. She collapsed in the foyer, crying and still clutching at her stomach. She felt a cramping pain so intense it nauseated her. The sensation made her dry heave. With one hand over her mouth, she pulled herself to her feet, and with a hunched back, wobbled to the bathroom where she collapsed over the toilet. Vomit spewed from her mouth as she fell.

She held herself over the commode, the tension in her belly tightened all her muscles as she spasmed. She felt a warm wetness between her legs.

Using the toilet for support, she pulled herself up to her knees where she could access the button on her pants. She pulled them down to find blood-soaked underwear stuck to her skin.

"No!" Iris let out a soft breath. Gently, with the tips of her fingers, she peeled her underwear down, wet droplets of blood stuck to her skin like perspiration after a workout. She stood, an imprint in fire-engine red, like sponge art outlined where her thighs had been.

Deep crimson dripped from her insides and formed a

gelatinous pool around her feet. A guttural wail left her throat as she realized what had happened. She sobbed, her mouth open, fighting to let air in. A steady stream of liquid came from her eyes, mouth, and nose. The pain resurfaced and pulled her down again, making her squint and clench her jaw.

"No! No! No!" she screamed in between desperate cries and hard breaths.

Iris cried until she couldn't anymore, until all her tears were dry and caked on her face. The blood on her legs turned to a crust, and her heart hardened into a weighted stone in her chest. She focused on a blank spot on the wall as she let a feeling of numb nothingness wash over her.

The bathroom was small. So much so that she didn't have to move her head or take her eyes off the spot on the wall as she reached over and turned on the faucet in the tub. The water ran cold at first, it always did. She turned a knob to turn on the shower, grunted, got up to her feet, and stepped inside.

The drain stained red to pink to crystal clear as it carried away the blood of her unborn.

IRIS' eyes shot open in the dark. She gasped for air and clutched her belly. The pain was immeasurable. The soft outline of the moon's glow shone through her bedroom window, illuminating a dark spot on the bedding that surrounded her waist. The sheets were warm and wet on her thighs. She brought her hand down to touch it and felt gooey wetness on her palm. She reached her wet palm over to her bedside table and flicked on a small lamp, bathing the room in a warm yellow light. Blood. All over her. It covered the bed and soaked into the sheets.

Dizziness swept through her and she started to panic. Not knowing what to do, she stayed frozen. Infant breaths vibrated through her chest. As her heartbeat quickened, the bloodstain grew and her head became light. Her clammy skin stuck to itself and beads of sweat ran down the sides of her face. Nausea came next. The sensation overtook her, and she gagged clear mucus into her lap. She reached for her phone. Her fingers trembled as they searched the touchscreen. She found an escape and pressed the call button. The line trilled as she held the phone up to her ear.

"Another nightmare?" A groggy Sarah answered the call.

"Sarah... I need help. Please," Iris whispered in between deep gulps of air.

"Are you okay? What's wrong? Where are you?"

"Hurry!" was the only word she could manage.

Iris opened her eyes to a sunlit room. Beeping medical machines pulsed around her and an IV attached her to a cannula. Her clothes were no longer blood-stained. Instead, she was wearing a diamond-printed medical gown. She felt cold where the IV entered her vein. It made her body shiver. Sarah sat on the edge of her bed, holding her hand.

"What's going on? Why am I in the hospital?"

"Sweetie, you called me late last night. Do you remember that?"

Iris sat still in thought for a moment before she remembered the previous night. She met Sarah's eyes with a quivering lip and watering eyes.

"Oh, honey. It's okay. You're okay. I'm here with you." Iris cried into Sarah's shoulder, wetting the pajama top she was still wearing from the night before.

"The baby..."

"Shh, it's okay. The doctor's gonna come talk to you, hold on..." Without getting up or letting go of Iris' hand, Sarah leaned toward the door and shouted. "She's awake, nurse?" Sarah turned back to Iris with a soft smile.

A nurse walked in "You're awake. Good. Anything I can get for you?"

Sarah didn't allow Iris to answer and instead spoke for her. "Yeah, can you get the doctor in here, please? She just woke up, and she's confused."

"Let me get the doctor in for you," the nurse said to Iris before leaving the room.

"Ms. Callahan?" said a tall man in a doctor's coat as he entered the room, the nurse following behind.

Iris adjusted herself in bed to give him her attention.

"You've had quite an episode." The doctor kept his eyes locked on the clipboard in his hands, leafing through pages and paying attention only to the text.

"Can you tell her what happened, please, Doctor? She's right here, by the way, not on your clipboard."

The doctor put down the clipboard and focused his attention on Iris. Sarah half-smirked, looking pleased with herself.

"Iris, we're going to keep you on IV fluids, and you've been prescribed some heavy medications. You might feel a bit woozy and tired. That's all normal. We want to get you well rested here before anything else happens."

She nodded. Her throat tightened and she braced herself. "And what about..." Iris couldn't complete the statement.

The doctor looked to his nurse who looked back with concern; he cleared his throat. "I'm very sorry to say that there was nothing we could do. It was too late... the loss had already happened."

Iris burst into tears. She'd known it the night before but hearing it out loud from a doctor made it real and unavoidable. Sarah squeezed her hand a little harder.

"Thank you, Doctor," said Sarah.

"This happened because you are unwell, but we are here to help. Are there any questions I can answer for you?"

"Unwell? What do you mean, unwell? Was it stress?" Iris asked through her tears.

"Oh, you poor thing." The nurse said as she consoled Iris with sad eyes and a soft smile.

"I wish I could answer that for you, Iris." The doctor's face turned forlorn like he pitied her, and he and his nurse left the room.

Iris' tears became a deep sorrow that engulfed the space. The emotion they carried bled out into the hallway where passing nurses and patients clutched at their chests in empathy. The nurse poked her head back in, only to grab the door handle and pull it shut. Sarah held Iris for several minutes and Iris let go, her grief avalanching.

THIRTY-SIX

Iris cried herself into complete exhaustion. Her body sank into the pillows and the stiff hospital sheets. She let her neck bend until it fell naturally to the side. Sarah stood there, her presence was enough to comfort Iris.

"Can I do anything for you? Do you want me to call your mom? Elijah?"

"Oh, god no, don't call him. I can't talk to him anymore."

Sarah sucked her teeth and frowned. "Honey, I know it's hard, but it doesn't mean he can't be there for you."

"No. No, it's not that..." Iris closed her eyes and her voice trailed off.

"What is it, then?"

Iris shook her head, rousing herself, but took a breath to respond. "Every time I see him, I just run away. I can't face him."

Sarah nodded. "Well, I'm here for you then. If no one else..."

"I guess this is for the best, anyway, right? I mean, he's a murderer. I couldn't have a baby with him." Iris scoffed.

Sarah shook her head, and her face contorted into pity. "Speaking as your friend, not your therapist, do you think there's a possibility that you're confused? If he really killed her, or if the cops had suspicion to believe that he did, don't you think they would have done something?"

"Are you working together? With Elijah?" Iris leveled a deep and piercing glare into Sarah's eyes. She crossed her arms as a powerful fear gripped her, and she waited for a response.

Sarah laughed but sobered when she saw Iris continued to look fearful. "What? Are you serious?"

"When's the last time you spoke to Elijah? Did you plan all of this?" Iris was getting worked up.

"Sweetie, I don't know what you're talking about. I'm just talking—trying to help you figure out what Elijah said and what it means. Why don't we take some deep breaths?" Sarah started deep breathing and gestured for Iris to follow her.

"Don't give me that! You and your breathe deep crap!" Iris yelled. "Tell me what you know! Give me your phone." Iris lunged for Sarah and fell out of the bed, her palms catching the floor before she completely toppled out. Sarah jumped back, hardly missing the attack.

"Iris!" Sarah yelped. "Oh, my god, are you okay? Are you hurt?" Sarah bent over her friend to help her back up.

Once she was safely back in the bed, the room went silent. Sarah kept her distance from Iris and crossed her arms, looking at the floor. Iris kept her own arms locked in the same position and looked straight up at the muted wall TV playing the day's newscast.

"Whatever this is, Sarah. I will find out. I will," Iris said in an aggressive whisper. Sarah's eyes widened in surprise.

She opened her mouth to speak, but let the words fall away into nothing, staying silent.

A nurse came into the room. "Okay, we're just going to make an adjustment here," the nurse said as she went over to the IV drip, and injected another medicine into the line. As she squeezed down on the plunger, Iris felt her eyelids become heavy and her body relax.

"Wait... what's in that?" Iris said, but her voice was already low and slow. She received no response from the nurse who only looked at her with a half-smile. Just before sleep took her, she saw two uniformed police officers walk into the room.

"Everything okay in here?" one officer asked.

"Yes, she's drifting off now," said the nurse.

Natural light soaked the space through the large east-facing window. A Blue Jay perched on a tree outside sang to the morning sun. The hospital air felt light and fresh as Iris took it into her lungs. She was warm and cozy under the soft covers.

"Oh, good morning, dear. How did you sleep?" the nurse said as she walked into the room. Iris noticed her for the first time. She was an older woman with a bright smile and salt and pepper hair tied back in a bun. Her aura and the softness in her voice felt comforting. She reminded Iris of her own mother, which reminded her to call June.

"Morning? How long was I out?"

"Oh, you slept all day and night, like a baby. You must have really needed it."

Iris sat herself up in bed while the nurse took her blood pressure and checked the bag of fluids hanging from the pole. "And the officers? What did they want?"

"What officers, sweetie?"

"Yesterday, before I fell asleep... I saw you talking to them. What did they want?"

"Oh! Them." The nurse chuckled through lipstick-stained teeth and shook her head while she flapped her wrist in a gesture that told Iris not to worry. "I think they just had some questions for you, don't worry any about that, dear. I told them to go away, that you needed your rest."

Iris nodded and gave an awkward smile. She nuzzled back into her pillow and took a deep breath to calm her hard-beating heart. The nurse looked at her with concern.

"Don't worry, sweetie. They won't bother you any. I promise. I may be old, but I got a mean left hook!" The woman laughed at her joke and left the room.

Iris grabbed her phone from the roll-away tray next to her. Her face unlocked the screen to reveal several missed calls and text messages from her mother. June must have been worried about her.

"Hi, sweetheart. I'm so glad you called. How are you?" June answered the phone before a full ring could complete.

"Hi, Ma. I'm okay. Well, I've been better, I guess..."

"So, I heard. Sarah called. What's happened?"

"Oh, I've been in the hospital since Monday night or Tuesday morning. I don't know; I was out of it."

"What happened? Are you okay now? Do you need anything? I'll come now."

"I'm okay. I..." Iris paused and swallowed the tension building up in her throat. "I, uh... I lost the baby." Iris fought the tears, but the memory of her miscarriage brought them anyway. They streamed down her cheeks and soaked her hospital gown.

"I'm so sorry, sweetheart. May I come see you? I'm on that side of town anyway, I can be there very quickly."

"Okay." Iris sniffled and wiped her face.

IRIS STOPPED CRYING ONCE she hung up the phone, but her eyelashes were still wet when June walked through the door. A puzzled look came over Iris' face.

"I was very close by. It took me no time at all to find you," said June.

"Oh, that's okay. I'm glad it didn't take you long."

"So," June approached the bed and offered a reassuring arm to Iris, squeezing her hand and smiling at her. "How are you feeling?"

Iris walked her through the events that had transpired and how she believed the stress of everything had caused her to lose the baby. By the time Iris got to the part about the police officers', the tall doctor in his white lab coat and with a bright smile walked in, interrupting the conversation.

"Well, Iris. It appears your medication has been doing its job, and we've rehydrated you. We're going to discharge you into the care of your regular doctor, but continue to drink plenty of water once you leave. Sound good?"

"Yes, thank you, Doctor." Iris smiled at him.

"Okay, you take care of yourself, Iris. The best news is, you don't have to spend Turkey Day locked up in here. Happy early Thanksgiving." He smiled back at her and walked out of the room.

"Oh, thanks. You too," she responded and looked toward the window. The sun seemed to brighten in a purposeful show of luminescence just for her.

"I guess that means I can go?" Iris looked at June.

She pulled herself out of the bed to gather her things and change into the clean outfit Sarah had left for her the day before. The blood-soaked clothes she had come in with were in a plastic bag hanging from a hook on the bathroom door. A shiver crept down her spine as she grabbed the bag.

"I guess there isn't anything to hide from him anymore.

I should just forget any of this ever happened, forget about Elijah, take it as a sign to get away from him, right? Like you always wanted."

"No, no, sweetheart. What I wanted was your happiness. And I shouldn't have projected my insecurities about my past into your future. You need him now. What you've just gone through is incredibly traumatic and he has had time to deal with Marie's death. You can both be there for each other and heal together. And while you each help each other, you'll feel more secure with one another, if that's something you want."

Iris nodded and looked at the floor, her lip quivering.

"Is that still something you want? To feel connected to Elijah?"

Iris took a moment to think about the question. "Yes, maybe... I do, no... I still don't know." Iris swirled in her thoughts as she became overwhelmed by them. "But how can that be possible if he *is the murderer?*" Her voice tensed as she relived the feelings her visions brought up in her. The stress took over her, squeezing and twisting her muscles.

June embraced her; the pressure of Ma's body acted as a calming force. The women breathed together. Iris' heart rate calmed and the darkness she felt creeping in dissolved before it actualized.

"Don't you think one more second about that. The police know what they're doing, and they will handle any suspects. Elijah is a man who made a mistake, and it's confused you. If this is something you want, to give him another chance, I think you can forgive what he's done. The alcohol is the enemy, not him," June said.

Iris nodded and her paranoid thoughts resolved themselves under June's cuddle. Elijah couldn't be a murderer. She'd been his partner for so many years and knew all his faults. While he had many, hurting another human so violently could not be one of them. He hurt himself and his relationships. But murder? It wasn't something he was capable of. She saw that now. "God, I'm so glad you're here, Ma. I was going down a dark rabbit hole there."

"Of course. I'm only here to help." June smiled and rubbed Iris' shoulder. "Have you spoken to Sarah about maybe having a joint session for the both of you? Help you two come back to each other?"

A soft smile crossed her face as she locked her gaze and thought about happier times. She missed those happy moments with him and wanted them back desperately. She believed they could be happy together again. "That's a good idea. But I don't know, we may not be on speaking terms right now. I messed up."

June waved her hand dismissively. "Oh, come now. She knows better than anyone how stressed you've been. A quick apology will fix it."

Iris nodded, reassured.

"Good. Now, you mentioned those police officers…"

"I still don't know what they wanted, maybe to ask me questions about Marie? Oh, god this nightmare is never ending."

"Well, I wanted to tell you I heard on the morning news that they've arrested a suspect. There's going to be a trial and Elijah will not be the one in the defendant's seat."

"Oh, my god! That's amazing, why didn't you lead with that, Ma?" Iris shrieked. She laughed and cried, overwhelmed with happiness.

"I know, I know. I wanted to make sure you came to the conclusion on your own first. You're a smart girl. I know you don't actually think he could do such a thing."

Iris let happy tears fall from her eyes.

"Anyway, maybe they're here to ask you to take part in the trial or to tell you something else related to the suspect. Either way, it's all good news."

"Oh, that is all great news!" Iris hugged her. "We can finally move on from this."

"That's right. Now all you have to do is call up Sarah, apologize." June looked at her with serious eyes. "And have her set something up with all three of you."

Iris felt the shame of being called out. "Yeah. I know. I will."

Elijah's feet couldn't carry him fast enough out of the studio and into his car. The fight with Iris was enough to fuel his rage. He got into his car and let out a guttural scream, grabbed the steering wheel, and shook himself violently against it. He hated fighting with Iris, especially when it came to his mother.

"So, fucking what if I give her money for drugs?" he reasoned out loud with himself. "If I don't, she's just gonna do something horrible to get it from someone else. And if I tell you to go with her, fucking go!" Elijah yelled, having already removed himself from the argument, unable to say these things to her face.

He stopped and took a few deep breaths. Once calm, he reached over to the glove compartment and searched inside. He pulled out a tiny black box and thumbed the soft velvet fabric covering it. The diamond ring inside sparkled when he opened it. "So, fucking much for this." He scoffed, closed the box, and tossed it back from where it came. Sure, it would only be a matter of moments before Iris would come running out after him, he drove away and thought about what he was going to do next.

"Four fucking years! Four years!" He yelled to himself again, trying to convince himself that four years of sobriety and the clean life he had been living was worth more than what he was about to do.

He parked his car in front of The Tavern. The sign was different. They'd changed it in years since his last visit. The front of the building was slightly more weathered against the bright new neon lights.

Elijah sucked in a deep breath, exhaled, and slowly lowered his head against the steering wheel, taking a beat.

"Ma." Elijah straightened up with an idea. "Call Ma." She'd talk him off the ledge; he was sure of it. The line trilled. He waited patiently to hear her voice.

"Hello, this is June. Leave a message."

Elijah crumbled. He put his phone back in his pocket, and like a moth to a flame, walked toward the green glow of The Tavern's sign.

BY HIS THIRD WHISKEY, Elijah was stumbling and disoriented. He found this hilarious as he hadn't gotten this drunk from alcohol since he was a teenager. He walked to the end of the bar, looking for someone to talk to.

"Sarah?" Elijah said, surprised to see Iris' old best friend huddled in a girl group.

"Elijah! Hey!" She answered in an elated voice. Small world.

"What the hell are you doing here?"

"Oh, uh, just out with some friends for a drink. Are you here with Iris?"

"Huh? Na. She's uh… home. She's at home."

The toothy smile on Sarah's face replaced itself with a seductive grin. "Well, are you gonna buy me a drink, asshole?"

"Bartender! Shots all around." Elijah motioned to the bar, grabbing the barkeep's attention. A tray of shots hurried to the table, one for each of them at the table. They chugged them down, and the girls hooted out in celebration.

At some point in the evening, Sarah's friends made their way to the dance floor, leaving Sarah and Elijah alone. The conversation turned from friendly small talk to intimate and revealing.

"So? How're things going with you and Iris?" Sarah asked.

"Good. I guess. Have you talked to her lately?"

Sarah shook her head. "No, not since she moved in with you, really. What was that, like five years ago?"

Elijah nodded. "Yeah, I guess you don't know then that I've been sober? Iris' mom straightened me out. She's a cool lady."

"Oh, the best. Good for you! What are you doing here then?"

Elijah shook his head and searched for a response, already having backed himself into a corner. "We got into a fight. Iris has a big problem with how I respond to my mom. I walked out, and this is where I ended up." He shrugged.

"I'm really sorry to hear that, Elijah. I wish you would have thought to call me first. You know I'm always available to help."

"Maybe it was fate that you were here tonight? You and I have a way of finding each other and connecting on a deeper level, if you know what I mean." Elijah was flirting now. Sarah blushed and slapped him playfully on the shoulder.

"Oh, my god, stop. You're so bad!" She was drunk and impressionable. He was sloshed and broken-hearted.

The next moment the couple found themselves panting on top of each other in the women's restroom. Behind a flimsy stall door, Sarah reached into his pants and got him ready. When he was, she turned her back to him and arched, presented herself, and guided him to enter. When they finished, Elijah gently caressed Sarah's face and helped her gather her panties off the floor.

"Well, that was fun!" Sarah said.

"Can I call you later?" Elijah said, a satisfied and devilish grin on his face.

"You better." Sarah winked at him as she walked out of the bathroom to meet back up with her friends.

Back inside his car, Elijah sat in the silent darkness, his face stony. His eyes filled with tears and streamed down his cheeks as he thought about what he had done. A heavy sob followed. He searched for the ring box again, pulled it out, and looked at the sparkle that still seemed to shine, even though there was no light inside the cabin. He went over the years with Iris, her mother, and their bond. He smiled, pulled himself together, and drove home to her.

Iris paced several feet of her living room, with her phone in hand. She thought about what to say, how she would apologize. She and Sarah had been friends nearly all their lives, and she knew Sarah understood her better than anyone. Still, as the line trilled, an anxious rush coursed through her.

"Yeah?" Sarah answered.

"Hi, Sarah!" Iris said cheerfully.

"You make it back from the hospital okay?"

"Yeah, I did. Listen, I want to apologize for how I acted there. I was horrible. You were just trying to be a good friend, and I can't believe I did that."

"Don't even mention it. You're forgiven. You're dealing with so much right now."

Iris smiled. "You don't know how much I appreciate that. Thank you." Iris bit at her nails. "Um... I wanted to ask you something else. I'm wondering if you would agree to do a joint session with Elijah and me? I think it's time to tell him about the baby, and I wanna see if we can talk about a route to forgiveness. I miss him."

"Shared trauma is a strong connector and a way both of you can come to heal together." Sarah took a long pause before continuing. "Of course, if that's what you want, I'd be happy to do that for you."

"Friday after work, okay?"

"I will pencil you in."

"Thank you so much! You're the best!" Iris hung up the phone and danced around in her bathrobe. A new possibility of a better future on the horizon.

THE NEXT CALL she would make wouldn't be as easy. She knew Elijah scoffed at the idea of therapy. Over the years Iris had mentioned it to him more than once, and every time she was dismissed, defeated.

"Elijah." She rehearsed in front of a full-length mirror in her bedroom. "I wanted to call and say I'm sorry. I know I over—" Iris rolled her eyes at herself. "I'm sorry about overreacting the other day. I was wrong... Ugh!" She shook her head, shoulders sinking. "Come on, Iris, it's a phone call. You can do this!" she said as she stared into her eyes, looking at her stiff brows and determined glare. "Just call him!"

THE LINE TRILLED. Each ring that went unanswered only hastened her breath and brought the pounding of her pulse harder into her chest until her head and shoulders vibrated along in rhythm.

"Hello?" His voice caused her to freeze. Words escaped her. "Ii? Hello?" he said again.

"Uh..." she mumbled. "Hi, Elijah, it's me. It's Iris."

He laughed. "I know. Happy Thanksgiving. I didn't think I'd hear from you anytime soon after you ran away from me for the second time."

The sarcasm was not lost on her. Iris cowered. Her cheeks flushed red, and embarrassment zipped down her spine like an electric shock spilling through her veins and causing her toes to tingle. "I know, I, uh... I'm sorry. Oh, yeah. Happy Thanksgiving... Uh, I know the other day was weird."

"Weird? You accused me of killing my mom and then ran." Elijah's voice was stern, but there was a hint of a laugh.

"I'm so sorry, Elijah. I know you've been going through a lot. But I guess I have been too, and that's why I called."

"It's all good. I'm guessing you've heard the good news?"

"I did. They got him?"

"Yeah, so... I'll be dealing with that soon. Thank god. We can start putting all this behind us."

"We?"

"Yeah, we... as in you and me? I was hoping we could talk about us again."

"Um, well... I..." Iris hesitated. Not because she didn't want to jump through the phone and into his arms with a resounding "yes", but because she was forgetting the purpose of the call.

"I'm sorry, I'm sorry. I don't mean to be so forward. You said you've been going through some stuff too and wanted to talk?"

"Huh? Oh, yeah." Iris shook her head. "I just wanted to say that, um..." Her mind kept drawing blanks. The words she'd rehearsed in the mirror disappeared into nothingness.

"Ii, it's okay, you can tell me anything. What's up?" His voice soothed her like a warm hug.

"I just wanted to ask if you would come with me to a therapy session? I've reconnected with Sarah and have been talking to her about some stuff. She said she can facilitate a session together if you're open to it?"

"Oh!" He laughed again. "She did, huh?" he paused before responding. "That it? I thought you were gonna tell me something serious. Yeah, of course, Ii. I'll be there."

Iris let out a captured breath that released all the tension she'd been holding. "Really? Like, really, really? Are you serious? You're not gonna call me a pussy or tell me I'm wasting my time on hokey pokey bologna?" She had a tough time accepting his willingness to comply.

"Well, of course you're full of bologna." He chuckled. "But no, Ii, if you need this, I need this. I'm there. Just tell me when and where."

"Who are you, and what have you done with Elijah!" Iris laughed out loud, partly in relief but also in disbelief.

"Haha, very funny."

Iris felt calm and confident when she ended the call with Elijah. She gazed at the picture of them on the home screen of her phone, a smile creeping into the corners of her mouth. It was a random picture they had taken after work one night. It had been a long day, and Iris had been having a hard time dealing with a client account.

Elijah was already home, had been for an hour, while she had stayed back at the studio to close and finish a few calls. When she opened the door to their apartment, the living room was dim, illuminated only by the light of various strategically placed candles. The scent in the air was warm, like baking vanilla. She recognized it as the warm vanilla-scented candle he'd bought her for her birthday that year. She searched the room, having forgotten the stress of work, and found his naked body lounging on the couch, a corner of a throw blanket covering his man-bits, and a look on his face that screamed, "This is a rom-com, not real life". She burst into laughter.

Elijah jumped up from the couch and sashayed over to her, pulling her into him and making her dance with him back over to the couch. She allowed herself to be pulled into the fantasy he had created for her. He poured a glass of wine for her, and after a few sips, she forgot all about the difficult client she had, and instead, cuddled into his arms.

Sarah stood against the kitchen counter and stared into a clear coffee pot and an empty mug. The black liquid dripped slowly into the carafe as she tapped her fingers on the counter. She grabbed several green packets of sweetener and ripped them open together, all at once, and poured them into the empty cup. The sweet dust wafted into the air around her.

"Good morning, and happy Wednesday to everyone out there in the greater San Francisco Bay. While everyone's cooking, baking, and getting ready for our country's favorite food holiday, we are happy to report that one less criminal is out on the streets tonight. Yes, that's right. A disturbing discovery for officers who've made an arrest for the murder of Marie Miller..." Sarah's interest was piqued when she recognized the name. B-Roll film flashed pictures of Marie and clips of the suspect being escorted into the police station in handcuffs while the reporter detailed the gruesome facts of the case.

"Hey!" Sarah shouted into her empty apartment. "Come see the news. Have you heard anything about this?"

Elijah emerged from the hallway, wet and half-covered with a towel. "Huh? What's up?"

"Look, they caught someone. Has anyone called you?"

Elijah looked at the television and studied the report. He shook his head. "Nah, I haven't heard. I'm gonna call the detective." Elijah searched for his phone. "What you got going on today? You going back to the hospital again?"

"No. I just came from there. She's fine. June's with her by now, I'm sure." Sarah said as she shook her head and sipped her coffee.

"Okay, just saying… Gotta keep up appearances."

Sarah rolled her eyes and nodded.

ELIJAH CAME BACK into the kitchen, dressed, as he was hanging up the phone. "It's true. They caught the guy. I have to go talk to the detective. See you later tonight?"

Sarah nodded and smiled.

"Kay. Bye." He leaned in and pecked her on the cheek, and walked out the door.

Sarah stewed at her dining room table, surrounded by her thanksgiving feast for two, as she waited for Elijah to arrive. Her face held pursed lips and a tight stare as she waited for a knock on her door.

Knock. Knock. Knock. "It's me, babe!" Elijah's voice rang through the door.

Sarah rushed with heavy feet to answer, swung the door open aggressively, and confronted him. "So, I talked to Iris again. She asked for a joint session. You agreed to a joint therapy session in MY office?" Sarah fumed.

Elijah scoffed. "Hey babe. Happy Thanksgiving. What's the problem?"

"The problem? Are you kidding me? This has gone way too far. There's no way I'm doing that. That is completely inappropriate and deceptive. You have been in my bed almost every night since you left her, and you think I'm gonna facilitate a kumbaya between the two of you so you can pretend to get back together? This is so unethical. I could lose my license! No!" Sarah raised her voice louder as she rambled, exciting herself into a rage.

"Babe, babe, babe. It's okay. Calm down. We have to do this."

"No! We don't, Elijah. Actually, we do not. Why are we still hiding? We can come clean. This has gone on long enough. It might be hard, but she deserves to know the truth. I can't keep doing this to her. It's not right."

"Do you even hear yourself right now? She's fucking nuts, Sarah!" Elijah said, matching Sarah's energy. "She fucking threw a glass whiskey bottle at my head the day we got engaged. I told you this!"

Sarah, disarmed, lowered her head and nodded, taking a deep breath. "I know... I know. I'm sorry, I just... It's so much, and I feel so wrong for hurting her like this. She didn't do anything."

Elijah pulled Sarah into an embrace and held her. "Listen, it's okay. I met up with the detective today. There's gonna be a trial. After all this is over, very soon, we get back to our original plan. Texas. Remember?"

Sarah nodded and frowned.

"We just have to hold out for a little bit longer. I'm about to close the deal on the sale of the studio, my brother's getting ready for us in Houston; it's all working just the way we planned. This is the last thing. Okay?" Elijah lifted the bottom of her chin up gently so that she had to look at him. He kissed her softly. Sarah let out a hushed sigh.

"I hope you're right, babe. I really do."

Iris cuddled up on her couch and sipped her coffee. The silence was broken only by a loud knock on the door, startling her. The warm coffee in her mug threatened to spill but settled after sloshing within the boundaries.

Another loud knock pulled her to her feet. She tiptoed to the door and looked out of the peephole. Her shoulders relaxed, and she sighed when she saw her friend Sarah through the glass.

"Jesus! You scared the shit outta me!" Iris said as she opened the door.

"Hi, hon, how are you?" Sarah smiled at her, but there was sadness in her eyes. She reached out her arms and rubbed Iris' shoulders. Iris mistook the gesture for a hug and leaned in just as Sarah backed away.

"Uh, come in..." Iris stepped aside and made room for Sarah to enter. "So, what's up? How are you here on a holiday weekend? You're not going home?"

"Oh, I just wanted to come check on you, make sure you're doing okay. How are you? Are you okay? Do you need anything?"

"No purse? Did you leave it in your car? You know a car got jacked last week."

"Huh? Oh…" Sarah shook her head and waved her hand in a dismissive gesture before crossing her arms.

"Um, you wanna sit down?"

Sarah looked at the couch but remained standing. "I can't stay long. There's something we need to talk about. How did the doctors treat you? Did they give you everything you need?"

"Yeah, yeah, I mean…" Iris shook her head. "We just talked about this. Are you okay? What's going on?"

"Have you spoken to Elijah about the trial? How are you feeling about it? Are you nervous at all?"

Iris felt disconnected from her friend. Her questions were strange, and she looked tense. "Nervous? About what? Wait, do you think they'll call me to speak? Shouldn't someone be prepping me? Or tell me what to say? I haven't heard anything. Have you? Is that what you wanted to talk about?"

"Right. Okay, well, I'm glad you're okay. As I said, I can't stay."

"Um, okay. Still on for our session next Friday? With Elijah?" The two women began the short walk toward the door, but before Sarah could respond, another loud knock interrupted them. "Jesus!" Iris jumped. "Why does everyone think they can pound on my door like they're the police?" Iris shook her head and let out a snort.

"Let's go!" A voice shouted, pounding the door at the same time.

"Excuse me?" Iris jolted the door open, enraged. "Who the hell do you think you are? This is my apartment!" Standing on the other side of the door was her apartment manager, a miserable old woman Iris hated having run-ins with. The short woman cackled and coughed and smelled of stale cigarettes.

"Oh, relax, princess. I was just escorting these guys here." Her voice was hoarse. "They have some questions for you." The woman pointed to the two tall, uniformed officers behind her. Without making eye contact, she walked away, saying, "Here you go, boys. Go gentle on this one."

Iris scoffed and rolled her eyes as the woman hobbled down the hallway. "God, that woman! I can't stand her," Iris whispered under her breath, turning back to Sarah.

"Okay, I'm gonna go," Sarah said quickly and pushed her way out, passing the officers who paid her no attention.

"Uh, okay. Bye... How can I help you guys?"

"Ma'am," one of the officers said, while the other stood back in attention, staring at the wall behind Iris' head. "We're here to inform you that there will be an arraignment for the murder of Marie Miller. We try to schedule these things within forty-eight hours of the charge, but considering the holiday weekend and the court's backed up, you'll have to wait. Scheduled for a week from Monday, December sixth."

"Um, okay. Do I have to come or something? Am I involved?"

Both officers looked directly into her eyes. She felt an icy coolness run through her body. "Yes, ma'am. You have to come. Consider this your summons." The officers tipped their hats and half smiled before walking away.

Excited about our session today, see you at 6.

Iris texted Elijah as she closed up the studio and prepared to see him at Sarah's office for their therapy session. The week was coming to an end, and she'd refrained from texting at all. Instead, she performed her duties at the studio and made sure to take care of whatever she had control over in his absence. She anxiously awaited a response, something to confirm he was in fact coming, that what she'd imagined as his enthusiastic agreement wasn't just that, her imagination.

When the reply bubbles didn't appear, she swiped the screen back to the message pool and scrolled down to the chat box with Sarah.

On my way. Be there in fifteen minutes.

IRIS PULLED up to the old Victorian. She looked at the glass door draped with metal blinds unable to see inside. It was a couple of minutes before 6:00 p.m. She sat back and lay her head on the headrest. She closed her eyes and took a deep breath, gripping the steering wheel. In one heavy and long exhale, she let out all the air in her lungs, readying herself for the encounter.

She focused on the sound of her heels clicking on the sidewalk as she approached the door. The slight crashing sound of thin metal blinds against glass accompanied the jingle of the bell attached to the door, announcing her entrance. She gasped when she saw Elijah, already sitting in the lobby and waiting patiently.

"Oh, you're here, and early at that!" Iris chuckled, hugging him.

"Yeah, it didn't take me as long to get here as I thought."

"Well, I'm glad. Thanks so much for coming. This is gonna be really good, I think."

Elijah shrugged, put his hands in his jean pockets, and bobbed his head a few times, poking out his bottom lip in a look of childish submission. Even in serious situations, Elijah had a way of making things fun, he was funny like that. She'd always loved that about him, and she admired that even now he could hold on to that special piece of his personality.

"Iris, Elijah." Sarah emerged from the hallway, announcing herself.

"Yup." Elijah chuckled nervously.

"Come on back, guys." Sarah led the way to her office and gestured for them to sit on the couch before sitting in a chair across from them.

"Thanks again for helping with this, Sarah," Iris said.

Sarah nodded and smiled graciously before explaining the intricacies of therapy and the concept of the "safe space" for Elijah. The anticipation of sharing her news, coupled with the anxiety of how he might react, kept Iris' heart thudding. She gulped down a lump in her throat as best she could when Sarah asked her to speak.

In a shaky voice, Iris revealed to Elijah the secret she'd been hiding from him. His countenance took on a paler hue as the words left her lips. He looked utterly defeated and broken. As his eyes filled with water, so did hers. He took her in a tight embrace.

"Why didn't you tell me?" he asked, whispering and still holding her tight.

"I wanted to. I swear I did. There was so much going on. You had just lost Marie. I was freaking out about everything. I couldn't find the words." She got louder as she spoke, choking on tears, panic creeping in. She drew in hard and fast breaths.

"Hey, hey, hey..." Elijah touched her chin, and with a light tug, brought her to look at him. "It's okay. It's okay. I understand. I'm so sorry you had to do all that by yourself. I should have been there for you."

Iris locked eyes with him, entranced. The world didn't exist anymore. "I'm so sorry I didn't say anything before."

"No, you did nothing wrong. You're perfect, Ii. I love you, and you're amazing. Thank you for trusting me enough to come to me with this now. I'm just sorry it had to come to this for you to finally tell me. I never want it to be this hard for you to talk to me."

A floodgate burst in her brain; her synapses swelled with oxytocin as she relished in his sweet words. Her tears subsided, and a smile brightened her face.

"You better tell me what you've done with the real Elijah." Iris laughed. Elijah laughed. Sarah held an objective scowl. "You've never been so sweet. I like this new you." She relaxed into the couch, detaching herself from Elijah's embrace but sitting closer now with her shoulders pointed toward him. He put his hand on her thigh and squeezed as he smiled.

"I guess I'm just finally realizing what I had and what I want."

Sarah coughed and grabbed her throat like she was choking. When she recovered, she said, "Excuse me, sorry. Little tickle in my throat. That was sweet indeed, Elijah." Sarah awkwardly jotted notes in her notebook.

"I don't want to be that guy anymore. Losing my fiancé, my mother, and now my baby..." He turned to Iris again, his gaze seemingly piercing her eyes. "I want to be better. I'll come to as many more of these things as you need me to, for you to see that."

"Thank you," she said, not able to get any other words out of her throat that had clinched shut with an over-welling of emotion.

"SO..." Elijah said, walking Iris to her car after the session.

"Yeah?" Iris looked at the ground and kicked at the asphalt beneath her feet.

"Listen, I was hoping we could get together and talk before the trial. I just want some time with you before things get stressful again."

"Okay, sure. This weekend?"

"Brunch?"

Iris nodded and smiled.

"You make the waffles, and I'll bring the orange juice?" Elijah opened her car door for her. "See you Sunday." He said as he kissed her hand.

"Oh, my god, stop!" She giggled and said goodbye.

Sarah's office bells rang with the sound of the chattering blinds against the glass. Five o'clock on the dot. She shook her wrists and fingers and stretched her neck from side to side like a fighter preparing to enter the ring.

"Hey," Elijah said as she walked out of her back office.

Sarah looked surprised to see him. "You're an hour early. The session doesn't start until six."

"I know, I just thought we should practice one last time. Make sure we got our story straight."

Sarah nodded.

"Hi..." Elijah paused. He smiled at her with his chin tucked in and eyes half-closed, a look that enchanted her and swallowed her up in a silent seduction.

Sarah's cheeks flushed. She smiled awkwardly and wiped her forehead in a nervous show. Was she sweating? No, but she imagined she was and pulled her hand across her face anyway, to be sure. Her eyes darted around the room. "Sorry. It's warm in here. Is it warm in here? Are you okay?"

"Huh? Oh, no, I'm fine." Elijah remained calm while Sarah cartwheeled in her mind.

"Okay, good. Come on." Sarah led Elijah back to her office, fighting with her blouse and pencil skirt on the way. She tripped on her heels, but she played it off telling Elijah to watch out for the non-existent divot in the floorboards. Those heels normally sat in her closet, collecting dust, a relic of younger years in grad school when all-nighters and Happy Hours ruled her life.

Elijah entered her office and sat on the couch, legs open wide, and stretched his arms out on either side.

"Please, make yourself comfortable." Sarah scoffed and rolled her eyes.

"Don't mind if I do."

"So, okay. Ready?" Sarah pulled her hand over her face like a theater kid preparing to enter character. "Elijah, this is a safe space. We can talk about anything and everything, but I will remind you, Iris called this meeting specifically to speak about the two of you and how you move forward."

Elijah looked sideways at her. "What's with the doc talk?"

She rolled her eyes. "Nothing. It's just something I have to do to get in the groove. If you want me to get through this, you have to play along."

Elijah raised his hands in a sign of submission. "Carry on."

"Okay, good. Why don't you tell me about what you envision for your future with Iris?" Sarah had donned the metaphorical hat that melted away any personal anxieties and brought her into her therapist's chair. This was her office, her domain, and she was in control. She pulled her notepad onto her lap and readied her writing hand.

"We really doing this?" Elijah scoffed."

"You're the one who wanted to practice!" Sarah almost shouted.

"Okay, okay. You're right. I wanna get this right. Wanna avoid any flying whiskey bottles this time."

"I always thought of Iris as docile and passive. I still find it so hard to believe she attacked you like that."

"Yeah, I used to think that, too. Honestly, I don't even think she was aware of it... her eyes were glazed, it was..." Elijah's stared off into a blank spot on the wall.

"Well, anyway. We obviously aren't going to relive that memory with her today. She thinks you two are getting back together." Sarah rested her chin in her hand as she waited for a response.

"You look sexy in that pencil skirt. First thing I noticed when I saw you today."

Sarah's eyes widened, and her invisible hat flew off in an imaginary wind. "Excuse me, Elijah. I'm afraid that's inappropriate for this setting."

"I'm sorry, I'm sorry. But I couldn't let it go unsaid. You get me goin', babe."

As her heart beat hard in her chest, she felt a tingle drip down her spine and concentrate between her thighs. "Elijah! Not here, please. She could be here any minute." Sarah was flustered and filled with warm energy she hadn't expected.

"I don't know if I can help myself." He stood up, holding her gaze. He approached her slowly like he was rescuing a scared stray dog on the street, except with a seductive saunter. She remained seated but didn't realize when her body relaxed and her thighs opened slightly like they were inviting him in. He stopped in front of her and put his hand behind her ear, nudging her to rise.

"No... we can't. I... this is...." She wanted to tell him, no, but her body responded to his lead. She rose from her chair and found herself allowing him to pull her close. Their breathing synced as they looked deep into each other's eyes. "We can't." She gave her last attempt.

"Can I kiss you?"

She didn't answer but responded in one fierce and fast movement, locking her lips to his and pulling herself harder into him. Passion streamed down her as she took him back to the couch, ripping at her clothes and his. The two of them became a fireball of craving as they disappeared into each other. The lovemaking was fast and hard, matching the thirst Sarah had felt for him in the first encounter they'd had.

They lay next to each other on the couch, slipping on each other's sweaty skin. Utter bliss kept Sarah from thinking, and she remained in his embrace until a vibration of her phone pulled her out of her reverie. She stretched her arm across his body to the coffee table where her phone sat.

Sarah panicked as she read the text message aloud. "On my way. Be there in fifteen minutes."

"It's Iris!"

FORTY-FIVE

The oxytocin-doused couple sprung from their inhibited state on the couch and into action. Fervently jumping up from the couch, they grabbed at strewn clothing and throw pillows. Sarah quickly put the couch back together, replacing the cushions and items with care.

Elijah finished dressing and made a sound, distracting her and grabbing her attention. "Uh…" he said.

"What?"

Without words, he pointed to the couch. Sarah's eyes followed his finger, bringing to her attention a giant wet spot in the middle cushion.

"Shit! Shit! Shit!" Sarah panicked, almost hyperventilating as she batted at the fabric with her palm, wishing she could wipe away the set-in liquid with her bare hands.

"Relax, relax. I got this." Elijah's confidence was an ever reassuring and overpowering force. He smiled and touched the small of her back. The sensation froze her in a wave of calm almost instantly. He picked up the cushion, flipped it, and placed it back. Taking a step back to admire his work, he crossed his arms and nodded at the couch. "See. I gotcha."

Sarah fixated on him as her hormones still wreaked havoc through her, causing her to revere him like a Grecian god. A halo appeared around his head, and an ethereal choir began to sing, surrounding him, and basting him in glory. Sarah shook her head and washed away the image. "Stop it. Focus."

"Huh?"

"Nothing... You have to go. She'll be here any second." Sarah pushed him forcefully out of her office and into the lobby while she took one more look around to assure herself the place was back in order. A last measure of caution had her open the window behind her desk, airing out any sex fumes left behind.

THE METAL BLINDS CRASHING into the door announced Iris' arrival into the building just as they had Elijah's. Sarah stood still in her office, listening at the encounter between the ex-lovers. The closed office door muffled their voices. The exchange had her gnawing at her fingernails.

Sarah took a deep breath, fidgeted with her clothing one last time, and exited her office.

"Iris, Elijah." Inside, her heartbeat so fast she thought it might burst. That would be an easy out she thought to herself as she willed her body to relax and ignore the physiological responses of adrenaline.

Pleasantries' over, she walked them back to her office, and as she did, found her invisible therapy hat and secured it to her head.

Iris spent an exhausting Saturday preparing for Sunday morning. She nervously scrubbed the baseboards and toilet, swept, vacuumed, folded laundry, and did the shopping. Her mother called, Sarah called, she ignored them both. They wanted to talk about the trial, but she had other things on her mind. Elijah was coming for brunch, and everything had to be perfect. As she wiped and disinfected, she imagined how he would walk in, standing tall and seducing her with only a smile. Her thoughts took her through the apartment with him like a dance, the two of them growing close again.

By the time she finished, the apartment was put together perfectly well and tidy. The sun had long since set, and it was time to sleep, but she was restless. She finally found sleep in front of a blaring TV in the company of a glass of red wine. A trick she'd learned some years ago when she found it hard to sleep waiting for Elijah to come home.

SUNDAY MORNING, Elijah sauntered in, standing tall, the seductive smile on his face just like she'd envisioned.

"Got your favorite!" he said, holding up a bottle of Brut champagne and a plastic grocery bag that held a jug of orange juice.

"Mimosas!" she replied and hugged him in the entryway. "Come in. I started breakfast. Waffles and sausage, your favorite."

"The place looks great without a dirty man living here." Elijah chuckled as he surveyed the apartment, perfectly staged like a magazine centerfold.

"Here, let me take that from you and pour us a couple." Iris ignored the comment, getting the champagne flutes instead.

"Oh, just OJ for me."

Iris let a soft smile escape her.

"Yeah, I just..." he mumbled like he was having trouble getting out the right words. "Getting back on that horse. Found rock bottom, didn't really like it down there." An anxious smile crossed his face.

"Well, I think it's great. It's just a shame you ever..." She stopped herself from finishing the sentence.

"It's okay, you can say it. I know. I'm a fuck up."

"No. Elijah, no. Don't ever think that about yourself. We all struggle with life. That's why we need each other to make it through. You're gonna get through this, Elijah. I promise." A soft, reassuring smile crept onto her face as she put her hand on his shoulder and gently squeezed. "Okay, let's eat." Iris clapped her hands and flashed him a huge grin.

———

BRUNCH WAS quiet except for the several compliments he paid her on her cooking. Domestic life was something she strove to master, believing that in some way, it might make him want to live that life with her and forgo the past life he'd lived in the bars, with other women. Every new recipe became another opportunity—a trick devised to convince him to stay at home. As if a casserole could taste better than meaningless and unprotected fun with a vagina he hadn't met before. She'd tricked herself into believing it worked. Maybe it did for a time. But not long enough. The remnants of the broken relationship surrounding her now were proof enough.

Iris gathered the dishes and piled them in the sink while Elijah refreshed her mimosa and his orange juice. Despite the impeccable food and a flawless apartment, the morning was not going as perfectly as she'd planned. It was tense and awkward. Time to break the ice, but she was at a loss for how to make that happen. The breakfast hadn't solved anything, and her nerves took over. Elijah took their drinks and disappeared into the living room, leaving Iris to fret over the dishes.

He turned on the stereo, and a familiar song flooded the space between them. It was theirs; it had belonged to them ever since the first night they met and danced to it in a living room full of drunk teenagers. The same song he'd played to propose to her not that long ago. A smile stretched across her face as she looked up from the overflowing sink.

Slowly, but with purpose, he approached her, singing the lyrics and exaggerating his signature silly, sexy dance that made her laugh out loud.

"You have like no new moves." She chuckled and shook her head, rolling her eyes.

"If it ain't broke." He shrugged, grabbing her by the hips and spinning her around toward him. She followed his direction without protest. They danced and sang and mocked their younger selves, the teenagers who'd fallen in love all those years ago.

The lyrics rolled off his tongue as he sang. He stuck out his tongue and performed for her.

"You're so dumb." She giggled.

"Ii," he said, holding her gaze. "You know something happened that night? Something between me and you."

Her heart jumped up into her throat, blocking her thoughts. She shook it off. "We hardly knew each other."

"Na, I know you felt something too."

"Oh really? Well, I guess you shouldn't have slept with my best friend then, huh?" she said joking and half-serious, gauging his reaction.

Elijah's eyes jolted wide. He began to panic. "What? What are you talking about? Why would you say that?" Pulled up close to him, Iris could feel his heart thump hard in his chest.

"I was awake, silly!"

Elijah's eyes still showed confusion and fear.

"At the party? When we met? You had sex with Sarah on the floor while I was passed out drunk?"

"Oh!" Elijah let out a relieved expression. "Hey, man! I was a horny eighteen-year-old. You shouldn't have gotten so drunk... it coulda been you. You coulda had all this." Visibly deflating, he ran his hands down his body in a sexy stripper pose. They laughed together.

"Ugh, whatever." Iris rolled her eyes and smiled, still swaying her hips as he held her close. The song ended, leaving the two of them enveloped once again in silence, except for the sound of their breaths. Elijah looked deep into her eyes until she felt his stare penetrate her heart. He closed the gap, bringing his lips to hers, and squeezed her body tighter into his. She melted into him.

"Is this okay?" Elijah asked softly. "Is this what you want?

Iris let out a soft breath and nodded. "Yes. It's okay." For the first time since the breakup, they made passionate love. The experience was all-consuming and as fiery as the first time they'd been together on the rug-covered concrete floor of the studio. Iris opened her eyes sparingly, only long enough to see him smile at her or nudge her nose with his as their bodies tangled themselves up in each other.

The scene ended in an explosion as they both climaxed in time, holding each other through the gentle pulses that raked their bodies.

"Damn," Elijah said as he unstuck their sweaty skin, pulling away only enough to separate their bodies. Iris shivered at the cool air that snuck into the space.

"You know," he said. "This could be the new us. We can do this. I want to be a better man for you. I know I've already told you that, but I mean it. What do I need to do to make that happen?" he asked as his steady hands pushed away wild hair strewn over her face.

Iris was still not ready to respond. Elijah smiled and leaned in to kiss her.

"Shower?"

Iris nodded.

He pulled himself up off the floor and reached out a hand to help her up. They giggled like teenagers in the bathroom as they washed away the aftermath. She wanted him to stay longer, but neither of them could continue to ignore the reality of their lives. The trial was tomorrow, and they both had to be there, ready and prepared. Elijah said his goodbyes with a kiss and one last embrace.

"See you tomorrow. I love you," he said as he walked out the door.

"Love you." She stood in the doorway and watched him go until he was out of sight.

Memories of yesterday's brunch with Elijah flooded Iris' thoughts as she rose on that Monday morning. It was the day of the trial, but she was unaffected by the weight of the event. She got ready for the courthouse and had her coffee, floating through her apartment singing old love songs and humming the melodies when she forgot the words. In front of a steamy bathroom mirror, she applied her makeup, pursed her lips, and batted her lashes. She made kissy faces to her reflection as she pretended to talk to Elijah.

"Oh shoot!" She said to herself out loud "Forgot to dish the bestie!" Iris picked up her phone and typed a message to Sarah.

It worked! I think we're back together! We had a beautiful brunch and sexy time yesterday. None of this could have happened without you. Thank you!

"Buh-bye!" she said to her apartment as she grabbed her purse and headed out the door. Why she did that, she didn't know, but happiness made people do silly things. Life was finally going right for her. Elijah had come back, she had told him about the pregnancy, her best friend supported her decision to rekindle the flame with him, and they were going to find justice for Marie. Why wouldn't she be happy and giddy and silly? She walked out to her car with a subtle skip in her step. The birds sang for her, and the sun showered a warm light on her.

A SMILE still stretched across her face when she entered the courthouse and walked through the metal detector. The guards scanned her purse and coat, tipped their hats, and sent her on her way. She followed the signs that led to the criminal courtroom and found her mother waiting in the hall.

"Hi, Ma!"

"Hi, sweetheart. How are you feeling? Doing okay?" The two women embraced. June looked concerned. She rubbed Iris' shoulder in a comforting caress. Iris could tell she wanted to talk about how she was recovering from the miscarriage, what was going on with Elijah, and if she was truly okay.

"Thanks, Ma. I'm okay. Really, I am. Thank you so much for being here. I'm really nervous."

"I know you are, sweetie. I wouldn't be anywhere else. Just to be here for you and to support Elijah." She paused. "How is everything with you guys? Have you spoken much lately?" she asked, being more direct than a look alone could convey.

"We're actually really good." The smile came back, and her eyes lit up as she answered. "He came over yesterday, and we had brunch and a nice talk, and... I think we're gonna work it out, Ma."

"Oh, that's wonderful news, sweetie. I'm so glad to hear that."

"Thanks, yeah. I'm thrilled. I mean, this is crazy." She motioned with her arms. "But despite all this, I think we're gonna get through it all and be okay."

"Wonderful!" her mother said. "Well, should we get in there?"

The women walked through the double doors of the courtroom, arm in arm. The mood shifted as Iris felt the eyes of a room full of people converge to her. There were no empty seats. People and flashes of press cameras filled the space. If Iris hadn't known better, she would have assumed they were all there waiting for her. The collective necks twisted to follow her as she walked down the open hall to the front of the room where two empty seats appeared, almost like they materialized from nothing. In the sea of staring eyes, she searched for a single pair that might seem kind or familiar.

"Elijah!" she said under her breath when she recognized him in the crowd. Finally, a friendly face. Only he wasn't. He looked different, older, like ten years had passed in the 24-hours it'd been since she last saw him. His eyes were cold and distant, and when they met with hers, they fell away to the floor in front of him.

Her mind raced as her heart dropped in her chest and into the soles of her feet. Her walk slowed to an almost stop as she tried to process his reaction to her presence.

"Come on, sweetie, let's keep walking," her mother said in a whisper and she felt her tug her arm. Her mother brought her, completely against her will, to the empty seat waiting for her.

"But... wait... Did you see that? What's going on? Why

is everyone staring at me?" Her chest throbbed. She felt her skin heat up and her mouth get dry.

"Calm down, sweetie. It's okay. Let's sit down." The calming, reassuring voice of her mother convinced her to sit. But inside, her mind reeled. She didn't understand why Elijah was so cold to her. With no other options, she took a deep breath and settled in her seat.

"All rise for the Honorable Judge Matthews," the bailiff announced to the room. The sound of shuffling and standing bodies filled the air.

FORTY-EIGHT

Distracted by her thoughts, Iris didn't hear the direction of the court and stayed seated as the judge walked into the room. Iris' mother, noticing the judge looking down from his bench and directly at Iris, pulled at her arm and forced her to rise.

"Ma'am." Judge Matthews' strong voice rained down over the court as he directed his address at Iris. "You will rise when the court asks you to rise." Iris was already standing, thanks to her mother, but the judge struck his gavel against the desk in protest anyway.

Judge Matthews sat back in his chair and disappeared into it as the back rose much higher than his head, his black cloak blending into it like a chameleon's skin, only the white hair on his head and the pasty skin of his face and hands separated him from it. Following Judge Matthews' lead, the rest of the court sat back in their seats.

Iris sat again, a new redness on her face. She looked at the floor, shamed like a schoolgirl who'd been caught in the girls' bathroom without a hall pass. She could hear only her breath and the beat of her anxious heart. Tension throbbed in her temples.

Her focus shifted, and she turned her head back to see him again, Elijah was looking right at her. "Elijah!" she called out in a whisper. "Elijah!" she called again when she didn't receive an answer. He looked away.

"Order!" the judge barked as his gavel hit against the desk three times. "I will have order in this courtroom." His scowl reduced Iris to the size of an ant under his magnifying glass.

"I'm sorry, your honor." Iris' voice made no more noise than the mice that might have been in the walls.

"Silence, you will not speak unless spoken to." Judge Matthews' face turned beet red as he expelled the air from his lungs.

Iris' mother put her arms around her and offered reassurance as Iris hung her head and silently whimpered. But it wasn't being shouted at that was bothering her. It was Elijah. She let herself drown in her thoughts as they grew into a sea around her. The current swirled and twisted and pulled her under. Adrenaline raced through her veins and pulsed all the way into the tips of her fingers and toes. Her vision blurred and tunneled into black. The sound of the gavel, still beating down against the desk transformed into the sound of shattering glass as Iris disappeared into a familiar nightmare.

Iris' mind transported her into a realm she knew couldn't exist, but found herself in, anyway. The room and the people disappeared, the bench where the judge sat stretched and gained height until it towered over her like a mountain. His voice rained down on her like a storm. She could no longer see him, but his voice remained omnipresent. Elijah's dead mother, Marie, walked into the spotlight. Her face was gray and bloody. The sound of shattering, cracking glass, the soundtrack of her life, amplified her fear.

"This isn't real!" Iris shouted out loud.

"Order! Order!" The ominous command and the gavel thundered through the sky.

The dark figure she'd wished she could forget stepped into the spotlight behind Marie and snuffed it out like a candle. The figure as he came into view, was Elijah. A sinister smile stretched across his face as he raised his right arm over Marie's head, who stood unaware but afraid.

"No! No! No!" Iris shrieked and cried. She knew what would happen next and looked away, unable to watch it happen. Iris' mother appeared and stood next to her, holding her so she wouldn't fall into the all-consuming darkness of her hallucinations.

"It's okay, sweetie. Calm down. It's okay." Before the relief could fully settle in, Elijah appeared behind June. Iris tried to pull her mother away, but Elijah smashed a glass fist down upon her head, her body falling to the floor causing Iris to follow her.

Iris held her mother's head in her arms as blank eyes stared up at her. Blood pooled around the wound. Terror poured out of Iris as she wailed. "This isn't real. It's not real! Ma!" Iris screamed and cried and choked on the words.

The judge's gavel hammered onto the mountain that made up his bench. His voice lost the harshness and became more human. The darkness disappeared, the courtroom reappeared. She hugged the air, reduced to a puddle of nerves on the floor. She shivered and sobbed as cortisol raced to every crevice of her body.

"Bailiff, remove this woman!" the judge demanded. The sound of jingling keys and boots rushed toward her. Two officers wrestled her to her feet and dragged her from the front row of the gallery. Iris' mother looked on with a gaping mouth and desperate eyes as they pulled her away like a stray dog.

"Ma, no... Help. Wait, Elijah! Elijah!" Iris continued to scream and fight as another officer came to assist. The two men pulled and tugged at her until they succeeded in their task.

"Don't look at her, don't respond, just let it happen." Elijah kept his head down and mumbled to himself as the scene unfolded. The rest of the courtroom gasped and whispered among themselves. Iris' boots clacked against the ground as loud as her screams. Elijah was forced to look back at the thump of the double doors bursting open and the officers crashing into them with Iris in tow. He caught a last glimpse of her fearful and confused face before they took her away. His heart sank in his chest as he ached to reach out to her, but there was nothing he could do for her now, and his mother needed him here.

Elijah turned back to face the bench. Without the distraction, it was time to focus on the bogeyman that sat at the defense table. Justice for Marie would be served today.

"Order! Order! Order!" The judge called for the court to settle. "This court will come to order." He banged his gavel on the desk, his face threatening to explode now. The collective gallery calmed itself and heeded Judge Matthews' demands.

"My goodness, we barely get through opening statements, and all hell breaks loose!" The judge gathered himself to proceed. "Prosecution may call your first witness."

"Thank you, your honor. Prosecution calls Elijah Miller to the stand," said the attorney, a tall suit named Bryant.

Elijah's chest tightened as his name rang in his ears. He took a deep breath, standing and exhaling before making his way to the witness stand. Under oath, the moment had arrived.

"Thank you for being here today, Mr. Miller. Before we begin, the court would like to offer our condolences for your loss," Attorney Bryant began.

Elijah cleared his throat and leaned forward so that his mouth was only an inch away from the microphone that stood out on a long metal rod wired into the wooden frame of the setup. "Thank you," he said, his voice cracking under the pressure. He coughed and adjusted his tie before sitting back in his seat.

"Mr. Miller, can you tell the court about the last time you saw your mother, Marie Miller, alive?"

"Yeah." He cleared his throat again. "I had stopped by her home because I hadn't heard from her that day. When I got there, this dude was there, and they seemed out of it." Elijah gestured to the figure of a man sitting face down at the defense table.

"What man? This man right here?" Attorney Bryant pointed to the defendant.

"Yeah."

"Please let the record reflect Mr. Miller is referring to the defendant, Mr. John Booge. Please continue, Mr. Miller," Attorney Bryant said.

"Uh, yeah, well. I already knew what they were up to. I'm used to it."

"And what is it you're used to, Mr. Miller?"

"They were high. My mom struggled with addiction."

"Understood. What happened next?" Attorney Bryant looked toward the jury while he spoke and rubbed his chin as if he were in deep thought or possibly antsy with anticipation about what Elijah would say next.

"Well, she asked me for money. But I didn't wanna give her any, I remembered a fight with my fiancé, well, ex-fiancé. She doesn't like it when I give my mom money, says I'm enabling her."

"Can you please tell the court who your ex-fiancé is?"

"Yeah, Iris Callahan. She's the one who they took out of here earlier. She's had a rough time recently; please forgive her."

Attorney Bryant held up his hands in surrender, speaking no words, offering the forgiveness Elijah asked for. "Please, what happened next?"

"So, we got into it. She was acting crazy, and then she just left with him."

"With Mr. Booge?"

"Yeah. They left."

"Your mother left her house with the defendant, Mr. Booge?"

"Yeah."

"And do you know where they went?"

"I followed them down to The Tenderloin. That's where she always goes when she's like that, and I mean, look at this guy, that's probably where he lives."

The courtroom erupted in a roar of gasps and mumbles. "Objection!" The suited defense attorney sitting next to the defendant rose to state his defiance. "The witness is making assumptions about my client that are unfounded and speculation."

"Sustained." The judge ordered. "The witness is reminded to speak only in facts and refrain from personal judgments about the defendant."

"Sorry, Your Honor." Elijah's heart thumped as his skin heated in his embarrassment.

The defendant kept his face down. His scalp was oily with long, stringy hair that hung down the sides of his head. An orange jumper clothed his body, revealing only his hands that were dark with scabs and scuffs. The black line of dirt under his fingernails was so thick, the rest of his nail bed was a gradient into gray. Elijah's face turned to disgust when he noticed.

"Thank you, Mr. Miller. Just to clarify, for the jury, that was the evening of Thursday, November 11th, 2021, correct?"

"Uh... Yeah."

"And the following evening, when you couldn't find your mother, the evening of Friday, November 12th, 2021, what did you do?"

"I went back to The Tenderloin looking for her, and him, kinda." Elijah pointed at the man. "I didn't find my mom, but I found him. I followed him to a back alley—kept my distance. He stopped to talk to a dealer, and I overheard what they were saying."

"And what did they talk about, Mr. Miller?" Attorney Bryant became animated in his expressions as he threw his arms up in the air and faced the jury.

"He confessed. He said he did it. He said he bashed her head in. I knew he was talking about my mom."

The courtroom responded with gasps and hushed whispers.

"Order!" The judge banged his gavel.

"Ladies and gentlemen of the jury, you heard it with

your ears. Mrs. Miller's son followed this man." He pointed to the defendant, still glazed in stone in his chair. "This man, who was the last person to be seen with Marie alive, admitted to killing the woman by bashing her head in. We will spend the rest of this session showing you the evidence that verifies Mr. Miller's testimony. Thank you, Mr. Miller. Your Honor, no further questions."

As the trial proceeded, Attorney Bryant did for the jury what he promised. By the end, Elijah felt conviction in his belief that his mother was, in fact, murdered by the dark character sitting at the defense table. The case felt airtight, he thought, as he sat back in his gallery seat in a comfortable lounge, knowing they wouldn't call on him again.

IT WASN'T until the jury retired for deliberation that Elijah felt his nerves tighten. He sat up straight and shuffled his hands, breaking only to wipe beads of sweat from his brow or loosen his already slack necktie.

Elijah sat quietly stewing in his anxiety until the jury reappeared and took their assigned seats. The pageantry continued, and the judge recited the words required for the jury's verdict. Of all of them, the only word Elijah heard was juror number one as they announced, "Guilty!"

The fanfare was minimal. The court officers escorted the defendant, who was no one to anyone, away. Elijah released his breath and a single tear. He was alone. There was no one left to celebrate with. The gallery slowly emptied.

"Elijah?" He felt a soft hand on his shoulder and looked up.

"Ma!" He stood up quickly and pulled her into a firm

embrace. The touch was more than his strength could bear, and he disintegrated in a fit of chest-heaving sobs as she held him.

"Oh, it's okay, sweetie. I'm right here."

His sobs wet her shoulder as he buried his head deep into it.

"I am right here, don't you worry."

He took in deep breaths to gain his composure. "Thanks, Ma. Thanks for being here."

"Of course, I'll always be here. You know I love you like a son. I'm so happy we got justice for Marie today."

"Yeah." Elijah nodded and wiped his face. "Is Iris okay? What happened?"

"Oh, yes. That silly daughter of mine. She'll be fine. She's had a rough go of it lately. I think she was confused today. But I'm sure she's okay now. Why don't you call her and tell her the good news?"

"Yeah, I will. Thanks. Um... Thanks again for being here. It really means the world to me that you came."

"Of course, sweetie. Let's have dinner soon. I have a few things at the house that could use fixing."

Elijah chuckled. "Anything for you, Ma. I gotta go. Love you. I'll stop by next week, normal time."

"Okay, love you too, sweetie, bye-bye."

FIFTY

The air outside was crisp and bright. The buzz of men and women in black suits strutting past as they had somewhere to be released an aura into the atmosphere. Everything was alive and bustling. He pulled out his phone, craving to text her.

"The trial's over. Where are you?" he typed and waited for the bubbles to reveal she was texting back.

"Elijah, I can't do this with you. It's over. Please do not contact me again." Sarah responded.

"What? Sarah, please! Why are you doing this?" Elijah waited.

"I know you spent the day with her on Sunday. Did you think I wouldn't find out? I'm the best friend! Idiot!"

Elijah panicked and dialed her number.

"What?" she answered aggressively.

"Sarah, come on. What did she tell you? All I did was talk to her about the trial. We discussed this. All part of the plan, remember?"

"I'm not stupid, Elijah! You're playing both sides, and

I'm not just gonna sit around like a lost puppy and wait until you make up your mind."

"It's not like that. Can we talk about this in person?"

"No! Where's Iris? Wasn't she at the trial with you?"

"That's also something we should talk about. Something happened. I'll tell you everything, but please, let's just meet up, please."

The line went silent for a moment. "Meet me at the Coffee House on the corner of Main and First. Fifteen minutes."

"Oh, I can come closer to you? Are you at your office?"

"NO! Main and First."

Elijah laughed out loud before responding. "Joking, see you in fifteen."

FIFTY-ONE

Elijah scanned the Coffee House. Sarah was easy to find, despite her table being tucked away in a corner and out of sight. When he approached, she sat up straight and tall in her seat.

"Thanks for meeting me," Elijah said as he pulled out his chair and sat down.

"You said you had something to tell me?" Sarah was short with him. Elijah's face recoiled. He was surprised that his charm wasn't working on her, at least not anymore.

"Uh, yeah, okay. I just thought we could talk too?"

"There's nothing for us to talk about. What happened between us was a mistake. I lost control of the situation, and not only was it completely unprofessional, but it all goes against everything I believe in about loyalty and relationships. I'm a god damn family therapist, for Christ's sake!" Sarah dropped her head and sighed. "I wish I'd never ran into you at that fucking bar."

Elijah sat back in his chair. "So that's it then? These last few weeks and all our plans out the window? What about Texas?"

"What about it? You really think I'm gonna run away with you to Texas? You found me at a low point in my life. It was a mistake. This is stupid. We're not teenagers who can just decide to run out on our lives. We're done. Do you understand?"

"Come on, Sarah! By the time we happened, you hadn't even spoken to her in years! What? You went to a few Marg Meet Up's, had a kumbaya girl's weekend at the Bay, and now you're feeling guilty?" Catching his tone, he settled himself before continuing. "We got a little derailed, but that doesn't mean this was never supposed to happen. Doesn't mean what we have isn't real." Elijah took a beat. He reached across the table to grab Sarah's hand. Her face softened at his touch.

"Elijah." Sarah spoke his name clearly and sternly, like a mother scolding a child for running around with scissors. Her face stiffened again. "Tell me you understand."

Elijah shook his head, took his hands away, and rubbed his eyes with his fingers like he was kneading the moisture out of them. "Yeah. Got it."

"Good. Now, what happened in court with Iris?" Sarah sat back in her chair with her arms crossed.

"Look, Sarah. I just don't know if I can stop with you. I can't stop thinking about you. You can't say all of this was just a mistake. It was more than that. I know you felt it too. Don't say you didn't."

Sarah sighed and dropped her chin to her chest. "Elijah, it doesn't matter what I feel." She leaned in to whisper the next sentence. "I could lose my license. This is irredeemable. It can't happen. I encourage you to refocus on your relationship with Iris as she is under the impression that the two of you are getting back together—or are back together. Isn't that true?"

"Sarah, please." Elijah hung his head and covered his face. "I don't know what I'm doing."

Sarah's face softened, and she reached out to touch his arm. "Elijah, I understand what you're going through is so, so difficult. But this is exactly why you need to grab onto Iris. You have an opportunity to heal with her and restart. She's the only person who can relate to what you're going through right now. You can build each other back up and start over. I'm the one who never should have stepped in and got involved. I'm the reason you're confused, not her."

He sniffled. "You're right."

"You're good for each other if you let her in and stop pushing her away."

He nodded. "I'm worried about her. She had a meltdown in court. Started screaming and thrashing on the floor. They carried her out. I don't know where they took her."

"What do you mean, you don't know? You didn't call her?"

"She wasn't there when I came out. You were the first person I contacted."

Sarah let out a labored sigh. "Jesus, Elijah. Okay, I will try to find out more. Thank you for telling me. In the meantime, you go home, relax. Congratulations on the trial. I'm very happy that you're finally able to move on from this. I have to go." Without waiting for him to say goodbye, Sarah stood and rushed out of the cafe, leaving him behind with his elbows on the table and his head hanging between his shoulders.

He sat there a moment to collect himself before he stood and walked out. As he reached the door, his phone beeped. A message notification lit up the screen. The words, "Message from Sarah," ran across it.

"Excuse me!" an annoyed customer trying to leave the building called out, Elijah blocking his exit.

"Huh? Oh, sorry." He stepped out and allowed the man to pass. Refocused on the message, a smile swept across his face, and he breathed out a sigh of satisfaction.

Iris rummaged through her refrigerator, skipping prepared meals of deli meats and bite-size veggies. It was late in the afternoon by the time the officers let her out of custody, and she made the trek home from court. She'd missed lunch, but she wasn't hungry. Instead, her arm jolted to an open half-empty bottle of wine. The whole morning had been traumatic. Having to explain away her behavior to the on-call court psychologist as stress, due to lack of sleep, had been exhausting and ruined her appetite. Yes, wine was exactly what she needed now.

She ignored the calls and texts from her worried mother. That conversation wasn't one she was ready to have. Her stomach turned and twisted into knots as she recalled the events of the court experience like a broken record. She told herself she didn't care, and it didn't matter. The only thing that mattered was that they had convicted the murderer. Guilty. It meant Elijah could be at peace. She reminded herself of the reason she was even doing any of this. All for him. Always for him.

"Oh, Elijah!" she said out loud as she emptied the left-over bottle of wine into a glass built for Iced Tea. What had happened? Why had he ignored her? The thoughts tormented her the same now as they had hours earlier in the courtroom.

She took a long gulp from her glass. The liquid, albeit cold, did not go down smoothly. Her body shivered as the drink hit her empty stomach. Once the feeling passed and replaced itself with mild euphoria, she took another gulp, hoping the next one would bring on a relaxation strong enough to push Elijah out of her mind completely.

"He's fucking cheating on me." She directed her words at the imposter wine cup, then laughed a little. "Ugh, whatever!"

"IRIS!" Iris listened to frantic voicemails from Sarah. "What happened? Are you okay? Are you home? Can I come see you?" the recording of Sarah's voice said. Her face curled into disgust as she lounged on the couch, her tongue and lips stained with wine.

"How does this *she* know what's going on?" she asked her phone. Curiosity got the best of her. She called Sarah back.

"Iris, you're okay. Thank god. Are you okay?" Sarah asked, still feverish.

"Hi." Iris' eyes squinted with skepticism. "Thanks for checking on me. I'm fine. The court was weird."

"Do you wanna talk about it?" Sarah responded.

"I guess...wait. Do you know already?"

The line stayed silent.

"Hello?" Iris questioned as her voice tightened.

"Iris..." Sarah cleared her throat and gave herself time to

think. "Your mother called me. She was worried. What happened?"

The answer didn't satisfy, but she needed someone to talk to, the release from the wine already fading as her memories of the morning consumed her. "I just don't think I have a handle on these nightmares. They're getting worse. Elijah was acting weird too. After the day we had yesterday, it just didn't make sense. He told me he loved me, and now he's ignoring me."

"Well, that was hours ago. Have you talked to him since?" Sarah asked.

"No. Not since."

"Understand that this was a highly emotional day for him too. It's likely his mind was elsewhere, and he was distracted by the trial."

Iris felt a shift in the air. It was like her nose could suddenly smell suspicion, and it was all-encompassing. It overwhelmed her faculties and drowned out her breath. "Why are you on his side all of the sudden? You weren't there. You don't know what happened."

"Iris, I understand you're stressed..."

"Stressed, I'm stressed, I'm always stressed." Iris interrupted. "Do you even know any other words? You're always defending him. Why? Have you talked to him behind my back? What's really going on here, Sarah?" Iris felt her body become hot and her chest tighten. She stood and paced around her living room, and her voice grew loud as she continued. "You know what. Don't answer that. I told you already I would find out what's going on here. Don't call me again!" Iris smacked down the phone. But it wasn't satisfying enough.

Little Iris watched her mother as she smashed the phone down on the receiver after an emotional call from her father.

It was the sound. Like anger turned to song. She needed it. Cocking her arm back behind her head, she released the phone into the air. It hit a framed art piece. The sound of glass and metal as it crashed hard against the wall pulsed through her like it had relieved an itch too deep to scratch.

FIFTY-THREE

She wouldn't let him do this to her again. Something was going on, and she wouldn't sit idly by and wait for her life to implode on her. The first time he left was hard enough. She couldn't survive it a second time. Gone were the days of her lying in a meadow like a baby fawn who waits for its mother to come back and tell her it's safe to move again.

This sense of confidence and power poured into her, and a light bulb lit up her thoughts. She grabbed her computer. A Google search pulled up a list of "private investigators near me" and she began her research. The first number she called went to voice mail. The second disconnected. The third was out of service. Each attempt left her more frantic and desperate. On the fourth try, an ad for a company called Cheaters and Liars promised 'fast results for a more restful sleep!' The line trilled. By the fifth ring, her confidence deflated. But then a deep voice answered the call.

"Paul the PI, Cheaters and Liars, how can I help?"

"Hi, Paul. My name's Iris... uh, yeah. Just Iris. I'm wondering if you can help me?"

"Shoot!"

"I'm trying to figure out what my fiancé is up to. He's been acting weird lately, and I think he may be involved with another woman, again. I need to know for sure. Can you help me?"

"I will be happy to!" His response was overzealous. She imagined he must really love his job.

Iris divulged intimate details of their relationship, and without offering too much information about herself, she gave up personal information about Elijah that might help the investigator track him. Paul assured her that if anything was going on, he would find it and she'd be sleeping easy again.

"Well, I'm very glad you called, Miss. This guy sure sounds like a sleazeball, and I'm happy to help you. There is the matter of my fee to discuss."

"Right, right... What do you charge?"

"Well, you've given me plenty to go on. And it's not as if this guy is hiding or missing, so he should be easy to find. A job like this will take about a week. If you want hard evidence and pictures, I charge $150 an hour, and I work full time. So, we're talking five workdays, times eight hours a day... That's gonna get you at $6,000, and that will come with all the pictures, videos, hard evidence you need. If he's in his home, I can only take pictures from the street. If he's a real scumbag and does something in a public bathroom somewhere, you might get lucky, but other than that, if you want me to go inside and plant surveillance, that's an extra $5,000. Call it hazard pay."

"Oh! Wow. Okay, um, no, I don't think we need to go that far. He does frequent bars a lot..."

"Sounds good. We might catch him in the act! Now, I need you to be on call. Stay close to your phone. If I get him in a position where a confrontation can take place, I will call and tell you where to go. Be ready. Sometimes these things happen quick. I'll keep you updated and send you evidence as I receive it. Sound good?" He was so enthusiastic, it was unsettling.

"Okay, thanks, Paul. Talk to you soon."

After the call, Iris walked back into the living room where her muted TV played a photo reel of memories from her camera roll. She plopped down on the couch and sat in silence while she fidgeted with her fingernails, her knee bouncing. She scrolled through images of her and Elijah. Each one felt like the sting of a needle pushed deeper into her chest. She gulped the rest of her wine and leaned back, exhaling her frustrations.

The next several days passed in a haze. She didn't go to work, didn't answer her phone, or leave her apartment. Sarah called. Her mother called. Even Elijah called. All of them went unanswered. She offered only brief text responses, enough to keep them from coming to check on her. A text told them she was alive, and that would have to be enough. She told Sarah she was taking personal time and would miss Marg MeetUp as if their last conversation had never happened. She explained to her mother that she wasn't feeling well and took some time off work to recharge and recover.

It was only a matter of time before Paul would come back with evidence that would confirm her fears. She needed something to prove that her episode in the courtroom wasn't for nothing, that she wasn't crazy or paranoid or imagining things. No one had said these words to her, but she knew they were all thinking it.

Elijah's calls and texts were the hardest to ignore. When he reached out, a sting in her chest welled up and brought tears to her eyes. She ached for him to be near her, but she wouldn't be made a fool, not again.

Hey, Ii. Just checking in.

Everything okay?

Can I bring you anything?

The messages were punctuated by several missed calls; she had to respond.

I'm fine. Sorry, boss. I haven't been feeling well, I won't be back at the studio for a while.

No problem. Take all the time you need. I haven't seen you since the trial, and I just wanted to make sure you're okay. Can I come over tonight?

Her heart swelled in her chest and clogged her throat. She typed her response.

Not tonight. As I said, I'm not feeling good. I'm sure you could find something better to do, anyway.

She wanted to type 'someone' instead of 'something', but she was afraid the pettiness of such a statement would tip him off, she had to be careful.

What is that supposed to mean? Did I do something wrong?

Iris felt his concern, which only intensified the pain in her heart.

Nothing. No, I'm sorry. I'll call you in a couple days.

There would be a confrontation. The $6,000 she paid to a private investigator would guarantee that. But until she had all the information, she would stay hidden in her apartment, away from the people that loved her, tangled up in her thoughts. Iris fixated on her hired gun, Paul the PI. She waited for his investigation report. Elijah wouldn't be able to hide anymore, and as soon as she had the evidence, she would confront him.

Iris wandered through her apartment like a ghost—if

ghosts wore white robes and fuzzy slippers and their hair tied back in a messy bun. She mumbled to herself, talked to the framed photos on the walls, and joked with herself that maybe she was going crazy.

THAT EVENING, her phone buzzed. It was the notification she'd been waiting for. Paul the PI popped up on the caller ID. She couldn't answer fast enough. She fumbled and dropped her phone.

She picked up the phone from the floor and screamed before she even brought it up to her ear. "Hello! Hello!"

"Miss Iris. Hi. It's Paul. How are you this evening?"

"Hi, good. Hi..." Her nerves tingled and her pulse raced. "You got anything for me?"

"I do, actually. Now, before we get started, I wanna tell you that I've followed this guy all week. And, well, this is the worst part of the job, because I'm afraid I have some bad news."

"What?" She braced herself.

"Well, he's exactly who you suspected him to be. A scumbag. I hate to say it, I'm sorry."

Iris let out a sad breath of relief. "Oh... okay. What did you find?"

"I'm emailing you my report now. I can go over it with you. But basically, he's been seeing another woman. I followed her as well. She's a therapist, has an office downtown. He frequents the office, and she's even been to his home once this week."

Her hands trembled and she covered her mouth.

"Now, there's more information and photo evidence in the report, but before we get stuck in the weeds here, I wanna tell you I've followed Elijah to a bar by his studio. And, well, I was just gonna take some photos, but this lady showed up. They're both here now, so if you wanted to confront him, now would be the time."

Iris took a moment and thought about the ramifications of such an action. She imagined him standing, caught like a deer in headlights, beer in his hand and thumb up his ass. She would tower over the both of them, in a position of power. It was exactly the opportunity she'd been waiting for all week.

"A bar?" her voice pitched. "So much for not drinking anymore, asshole," she mumbled under her breath, forgetting someone else was listening.

"What was that?"

"Huh? Nothing. Okay. Yeah. Where are you? What bar?"

"I won't be here when you get here. I can't be involved, but I'll wait until you arrive to make sure they don't leave. I'm at 4430 E. Salem St., downtown. You know it?"

"The Tavern." Her tone was disgruntled. "Wow. He doesn't even have the decency to hide it." She felt the betrayal and shook her head.

"I'm sorry, Miss Iris. As I said, this is the worst part of my job, but it's what you're paying for."

"Yeah, got it. Thanks. I'm within walking distance. I'll be there in five minutes."

"Alright, I'll be watching. You won't see me, but I'll wait until you get here, then I'm off."

"Thanks."

FIFTY-FIVE

The gruff night air drew a breath out of her mouth like smoke from a dragon's lungs. She tightened her scarf and covered her face as she walked. The Tavern was only a few blocks away. The walk would get her blood pumping and help her ready herself for the moment of the clash. Conflict was never something she looked forward to. She'd spent most of her life trying to avoid it like the scared little girl that hid from her father's rage. It was like that first year of their relationship, before she'd moved in and when he was still running wild at the bars. Pretending it wasn't happening was easier than asking him why she wasn't enough for him. It was a pain she didn't think she could bear. But losing him was worse.

Iris mumbled affirmations to herself as her stride quickened. Halfway to the bar, a homeless man with matted hair and torn clothes approached her, seeming to appear from nowhere. The sight of him startled her.

"Spare some change, ma'am?" he asked while he rattled an empty paper coffee cup at her face.

"Sorry, no. I don't have anything." She recoiled and

shooed him away. The man shrugged and removed his shirt. Scars covered his body. The sight of them frightened her more. The action was so bizarre. She wanted to get away from him and quickened her pace. She looked back and found he was now without pants too, wearing only socks over torn shoes. She gasped and picked up again with a light jog. The next time she looked back, he was gone, disappeared into an alleyway or a dark corner, probably.

Up ahead, the neon bar sign showered a green hue on the wet sidewalk below it. The sight relieved her and allowed her to catch her breath and refocus until she was impeded once again. A group of young college girls exited the bar and occupied the sidewalk as they walked up the street toward her. There was no way around them; they were a herd. The girls fumbled and tripped over each other, screamed, and shouted profanities. One girl held another up, and one stepped off the curb and wandered into the street. They were sloppy but intimidating. Iris didn't want to go anywhere near them, but she had no choice but to head in their direction to reach her destination on their other side.

She took a deep breath and squinted but kept her destination in sight. The screams got louder and obscener as she got closer until they completely engulfed her. Their faces up close were full of makeup smudges and strewn hair. But something was not right. These girls, their faces were not young and supple, but old, tired, and wrinkled. Their bodies, while hardly covered in tight mini dresses, high heels, and gaudy jewelry, showed skin that was paper-thin, gray, and riddled with age spots, warts, and moles. The tall one was missing an eye, the short one was missing her front teeth.

The cacophony of the women having fun turned to the

cackling of old witches standing over a cauldron. Iris panicked. Her heart throbbed, and she gasped for air. She didn't understand what was happening and forgot where she was. The firm grip of anxiety closed its hand around her, squeezing her tightly and slowly.

Iris screamed, loud enough to drown out the witches. Silence. Her eyes closed, she heard nothing else. When she slowly opened her eyes, she found herself alone again. The group of old women had passed and was a hundred feet further up on the street, still falling over each other and causing a scene. Off in the distance, they sounded like young women again.

Iris shook her head and whimpered. She allowed herself to bend over and rest her elbows on her knees before standing tall again. Upright, she puffed her chest, breathed out a few deep breaths of fog, and like a moth to flame walked toward the green glow of The Tavern's sign.

IRIS REACHED for the front door, but a bouncer stopped her from entering. The man towered over her like a mountain with muscles on his arms so large they almost floated in the air, unable to lay flat against his sides. A scar on his face stood out and made her cringe; she couldn't look away from it.

Iris fumbled with her wallet and pulled out her ID. The man looked at it, and without speaking, took in a deep breath. On his exhale, he let out a loud yell that didn't end. The power showered her with a warm wind that blew her hair back and made her shield her eyes with her arm.

Flight won, and Iris ran. She didn't stop until she was around the back of the building, where he couldn't see her, and she felt safe. Iris leaned up against the brick and took time for several respirations. She was aware of her surroundings and looked out for any boogeyman type that might chase her. Already having encountered a crazed naked man, a gaggle of witches, and a screaming giant, she had to be ready for anything.

Tears ran down her face. She sobbed silently to avoid attention from any other unseen characters that might be nearby. She shivered, pressing hard against the wall, trying to disappear when she heard it.

FIFTY-SIX

The sound of Elijah's voice on the back patio made her forget her fear. A gated wooden fence on the back of the building led directly into the outdoor area where bar patrons smoked or took refuge from the rowdy crowds inside. She couldn't make out the words, but she could have recognized his laugh underwater in a thunderstorm.

"Elijah!" she hollered. She took three bold steps toward the gate, only to be stopped by a man in baggy clothing and sunglasses with a half-dead prostitute hanging off his arm. He came from nowhere and stepped into the spotlight that shone over the gated back entrance. Iris gasped and tumbled backward as he came into view.

"Who you lookin for, baby?" the man said in a devilish tone and leered at her as if he knew something she didn't and was ready to act on it.

"Huh? No... nothing..." Iris tripped over her words. "My friend's in there."

"Oh, baby, I got something better for you than any of your friends do." The man's smirk spread out across his face to reveal golden teeth mixed with others the color of smoke-stained bone. Still hanging from his arm, the woman let out a tired laugh that sounded like a parrot's squawk. The man reached inside his oversized jean jacket and pulled out a large syringe full of a dark liquid. He slowly came at her, the woman in tow, the needle ready to engage.

Iris knew she was in danger. Elijah's laugh came again from inside the gate. With all the strength she had left, she screamed his name. "Elijah!"

The wooden gate swung open. There he was. Her shining prince had come to her rescue, standing tall with an equally surprised and concerned look on his face. Sarah came out next. Her shock immediately transformed into a deep sadness when she saw the scene in front of her. This only enraged Iris, who though felt safe was also reminded of why she was there.

"I knew it! I fucking knew it! You're cheating on me, again? With her!" The threat of the syringe disappeared from her mind, and her vision tunneled. Iris pointed her finger and yelled at a volume that pierced her eardrums. There was no reaction from Elijah or Sarah. They stood in the same position and with the same look, frozen in time. Confused, Iris paused, waiting for something, anything from them, but it never came. Not knowing what else to do, she kept yelling and pointing—needing something to happen.

The gate swung open again, and out came several men in white uniforms. The group surrounded her and restrained her. The ridiculousness of it all clicked something inside of her and she realized she was hallucinating again. She laughed at herself and rolled her eyes creating a bigger scene because, why not? None of it was real anyway.

"Okay, I can wake up now!" she yelled into the sky, snickering hard until she cried. The scary man with the syringe, and the whore stepped aside making way for Elijah. The man passed the syringe to Elijah. Iris rolled her eyes. "Oh, Jesus! Really?"

Elijah's hand, loaded with the syringe, reached forward and made contact with her shoulder.

"Oh, for fuck's sa..." He plunged the needle into her arm. Her vision blurred. Before she could finish her thought, her eyes rolled into the back of her head, and she fell completely into the capture of the men in white scrubs as her world faded slowly to black.

The first sensation she had upon waking was the tightness of thick leather straps holding down her wrists. She followed it to discover that the straps were attached to a metal bed frame that forced her to lie atop a thin spring mattress. A white sheet covered her body. White walls, white linoleum tile, and bright fluorescent lights engulfed her. She flexed her forearms, pulling and squirming for release but unable to achieve freedom. Her breath heaved in her chest as panic set in, but before she could scream, she heard a familiar voice.

"Iris, it's okay. You're safe." Sarah's voice filled the space.

Red seeped into her eyes and covered her vision in a bloody hue. Iris scanned the room, looking for the body that spoke the words. She settled on a chair at the opposite end of the room, where Sarah sat tall, her legs crossed and eyes staring straight at her.

"You!" The growl in Iris' voice was unnerving. "Traitor! How could you?" Iris screamed at her. "Help me." Her voice fell to a whimper. "I hate you!" she shrieked again.

Sarah did not move from her seat but reassured her that she was safe, everything was fine, and to stay calm.

"Calm?" Iris alternated between yelling, crying, and pleading. "How can I stay calm? Where am I? What happened at the bar? How long have you been fucking my fiancé?" The line of questioning was a disjointed purge of pent-up emotions, pain, and confusion. Iris continued to struggle against the leather straps and the squeaky bed frame, attracting attention from outside.

A white door with a metal wired window opened to let in two nurses along with Elijah who was dressed in a white lab coat and tie. The sight of him distracted her from her rage like a dog distracted by a treat.

Two nurses approached Iris. One placed a warm compress against her forehead while the other checked the straps around her wrists and tightened the ones around her ankles. Iris screamed Sarah's name and then Elijah's over and over again, aware, but unfazed by the nurses working around her.

"Sarah cannot save you now, Iris. Because she doesn't exist," Elijah spoke. She saw the words leave his lips, but the voice was not his own. Iris was confused. She'd heard the voice before, but where had it come from? The question was enough to stop her outburst. She cocked her head to the side like a puppy, eagerly wanting to understand its owner's command. Her mind calmed, and the bed frame settled. A nurse smiled and hushed her like an infant.

"Where..." Iris' voice cracked. "Who?" She paused as she flicked through her memories, searching for any clue of where she'd heard the voice before. "Elijah? The judge? Judge Matthews!" She mustered the strength to speak.

"Judge?" Elijah said and chuckled. "That's a new one!"

He bent his head down to jot a note in the notebook he held in his arms. "You are at the California State Mental Hospital in San Francisco. I am *Doctor* Matthews, your psychiatrist. Welcome back."

FIFTY-EIGHT

"No!" Iris shook her head and cried, fighting against the restraints.

"I'm afraid I am not Elijah, and I am not a judge." As he spoke, his face shifted like she was looking through an Instagram filter, unnoticeable until it had transformed completely. The face now matched the voice she already recognized.

"You are, you're the judge, I see you now!" Iris shouted. Her cries melted into rage. "What have you done to me?" She said through gritted teeth. Her eyes stayed locked on him, watching, waiting to see if he would transform yet again.

"You are mistaken, Iris. My name is Dr. Matthews. I am the head psychiatrist here at the California State Mental Hospital. I understand this is confusing, and I'm happy to explain everything to you. But first, I need you to calm down."

Iris grappled with her thoughts. What's going on? Where was she? Who is this man? What the hell is he talking about? Why am I chained to a bed? Where's Ma? A million questions swirled around inside her, exhausting her. She wanted answers, and she was too tired to continue fighting.

"Take a deep breath, Iris," Sarah spoke, still sitting in the chair on the opposite side of the room.

Iris glanced over to her, glared, and softly grumbled, "Sarah."

"There is no Sarah here, Iris. You and I and my two nurses are the only ones in this room. Take a few deep breaths and come back to me, please."

"What do you mean? She's right there!" Iris shouted at the doctor without taking her eyes off of Sarah, who sat still and tall. Her confusion was getting her worked up. She had no other way to let out her feelings. The doctor turned around and looked at the chair she was pointing at.

"Iris, there's no one in that chair. Sarah is not here, I assure you. You're suffering from a psychotic break that occurred after the death, well, perhaps it started earlier when Elijah sold his studio and moved out. Your brain, in desperate need of a way to cope, fragmented into different people and personalities, effectively inventing a new reality that allowed you to go on living a normal life separate from what has actually happened in the real world."

"You have got to be fucking kidding me." She shook her head and let out a derisive snort. "This is ridiculous, I don't believe this. You're holding me against my will. How do you know about Elijah? Sell the studio? Please." The rage slowly crept back in as a second wind blew into her, harder with each word she spoke.

"Iris, I am happy to release the restraints so we may talk more freely, but I again urge you to calm down."

She was at his mercy, and with Sarah sitting there smug and stone still, no one else was going to help her. Reluctantly, she took a deep breath and paused the thrashing, letting the rage seep out of her pores and fingertips.

"Okay. Okay," she said.

"Very good." The doctor nodded to a nurse, who responded by releasing her from the leather restraints, her wrists and ankles free. Iris sat up slowly and grabbed her wrists. She rubbed the red marks left on her skin where the friction from the straps burned her.

"Now," Iris said, her tone one of disbelief and cynicism. "What in the hell are you talking about?" She sat on the bed with her back coiled and her head low. She didn't believe him. She still had so many questions, but she would listen, even if it was only to end up laughing in his face and signing herself out of this place.

FIFTY-NINE

"Iris. You are a resident here at the California State Mental Hospital. You have been here since the trial when you were deemed unfit to remain in society for fear of hurting yourself or someone else. The judge appointed you under my care for the duration of your treatment, which, considering your condition, could very well be a long time, and perhaps indefinitely."

Iris closed her eyes as she tried to wrap her head around the information, but failed. "What do you mean my condition? What does the trial have anything to do with me? I still don't understand." Her breath quickened as she spoke, in tune with her rising heart rate.

"Iris, try to understand what the doctor is saying," Sarah interjected.

"You shut up, Sarah!"

"Ah, yes," the doctor began again. "Let's start with Sarah. Sarah, this version of her anyway, is a figment of your imagination. A coping mechanism invented by your mind to help you deal with the looming stress of death. She is not real, and she cannot save you now."

"But that's ridiculous. Sarah, tell him." Iris' response was calm and very matter of fact as she gestured with an open hand at the chair.

"Here?" the doctor questioned as he approached said chair.

"Yeah," she said in a tone that meant 'duh'.

The doctor smiled and walked the two steps back to the chair and sat down. Sarah didn't move but disappeared like a puff of smoke and reappeared an inch from Iris' face, startling her to a scream.

"You see, Iris? The only person in this chair is me."

Iris' eyes went wide, but she stopped screaming.

"Iris, I know this is a lot to take in, but he's right. It's time for you to see the truth now. I can't protect you anymore," Sarah's apparition said.

"But... what does that mean? What else isn't real, and what is? How much of my life is a lie?" she said aloud as her thoughts consumed her. This man in front of her had proved his worth. She trusted him. "Doctor!" She addressed him with a gleam in her eye that thirsted for answers. "Why? How long have I been here? What about Elijah and the trial and... please... tell me everything." Iris held her hands up to her face, desperate, like a lost child.

"Absolutely, my dear," he began. "Elijah leaving you was too difficult for you. We interviewed your assistant, Jessica, and gathered that's when you began hallucinating, but only sparingly. After the death, you snapped completely. Your mind shattered like the glass you used for the killing."

"Wait," she stops him. "What do you mean, I used?"

The doctor bowed his head as a frown crossed his face. "My dear girl, you killed..." He stopped before completing the sentence to rephrase. "You were anguished over the loss of your fiancé, Elijah. In such a heightened state of distress, people can become capable of unimaginable things. From the police report, we gather you were having a quiet evening at home with your mother. Perhaps she was visiting for dinner or just checking in on you. We can surmise that a fight must have broken out, and you smashed a glass vase against her head, killing her instantly."

"What?" Iris cried. "My mother? Ma? No, I didn't. You are wrong. I spoke to her just last week. She's been checking up on me." She couldn't believe her own words as they left her lips. Her eyes glazed over but tears didn't fall. She was in denial. Her chest heaved, and her breath broke and cracked as she began to choke on air.

In a flash, she was transported back to the night. But this time, it was different. She saw her mother; they were talking about Elijah and the pregnancy. She watched as the conversation became heated. She couldn't recognize herself, the bloody eyes and the flailing arms.

"This is when it happened," Sarah said, standing in the middle of the living room with her and narrating the events as they unfolded. "Your mother was trying to show you that the pregnancy test was negative. She reminded you that Elijah was moving to Texas with his brother and that you were confused."

Almost like a whisper, Iris caught pieces of the conversation between her and her mother. "He's selling the studio, Iris. What are you talking about being pregnant? Look, it's negative!" Her mother's voice rang in her ears like a distant memory.

Iris watched from outside her body like a movie as the other version of her grabbed her hair and screamed at her mother. "No, you're wrong, you're wrong, you're wrong!" she yelled and rocked back and forth.

"Honey, you need to stop this now! Get a grip!" Her mother's voice was full of concern and fear. Iris watched herself grab a decorated glass vase from a shelf, and without a second thought, brought the vase crashing down onto her mother's head. June fell and hit the floor as the tiny little pieces of shattered glass scattered on the floor.

"NO!" Iris screamed out loud as she found herself back in the white room, sitting on the white bed. The doctor and nurses stood beside her as her trembling chest breathed through heavy cries. One nurse restrained her, ready to inject her with a sedative, but the doctor stopped it.

"Thank you, Nurse Brown, but she's fine. She must feel this fully. We are breaking through the barriers of her mind; she's coming back to us." Hope colored the doctor's voice as Iris continued to sob.

SIXTY

"Are you ready for me to continue, Iris?" the doctor asked kindly. Iris took a moment to answer. She had murdered her mother. She couldn't fathom this. Her mind whirled with more questions.

"There's more? Who else have I killed?" Her voice cracked into a squeak as she braced herself for the worst.

The doctor sat next to her on the bed and reassured her with a gentle rub on her shoulder. The touch was needed, and Iris felt a slight relief from it. "After the event, I do not know what was happening in your invented reality, only you know that, but from the reports, we know you remained in a catatonic state in your apartment, with your mother's body, for what must have been days until your neighbor noticed a pungent smell coming from your apartment and called the police; they brought you to the hospital."

"My neighbor? No, it was Sarah who brought me after the miscarriage..." Iris' voice trailed off like she was in a daze.

"I'm afraid there was no miscarriage, Iris. Again, that may have been your mind's way of wrapping itself around the reality. We know Sarah must be important to you considering your visions, and perhaps a great comfort to you during this time."

"But girls' weekend at the Bay? Sarah and I reconciled? And Ma was there; this can't be right." A softness in her voice highlighted her naivety. She hadn't a clue.

"I'm sorry, Iris, but if your mother was there, we can assume this also only occurred in your mind."

"No! She's right here! This isn't right. None of this is right. Sarah, tell them. We were just at my apartment. You came to visit me." Iris groaned and begged Sarah to speak for her.

Sarah stayed silent.

Iris covered her face with her hands, her elbows on her knees. She wanted to curl up into a tiny little ball and disappear.

"Iris, you have not been home for quite some time. You have been in jail. There are records to show it. Before that, you were found in your apartment, in a catatonic state after the death of your mother."

"Come on, Iris," Sarah said with a gentle smile. "I'll show you. Come with me."

Hand in hand with Sarah, Iris was taken back to the day. Sarah helped her to dissociate the fake memory she held in her mind. Iris saw herself sitting next to her mother's cold, dead body. Blood pooled and dried on the floor and her clothes. Iris sat silently in a state of suspended animation. Her mind was bright and actively living a dream life that wasn't real and never happened. It was in this dream life that Iris reconnected with Sarah and Elijah, went to work every day at the studio, laughed, and drank wine. While her mind enjoyed the reality it had built in an imaginary world, her body stayed still on a floor covered in blood with her eyes glazed over and a half-smile on her face.

"When the police found you," Sarah said, still with her like the ghost of Christmas' past, "you were there on the floor, humming to yourself and rocking back and forth. For days you were like that." Sarah's words lined up with the movie reel she watched as the events unfolded. "They took you, you didn't put up a fight. At the hospital, you were evaluated and given the first dose of antipsychotics. That's why you remember being in the hospital, and you remember the police officers. This was the first time that reality broke through and into your fantasy. The two melded together briefly."

Iris saw herself in the hospital again, only this time, instead of seeing Sarah there holding her hand, she was cuffed to the frame, no better than a caught wild animal. The doctor and nurses surrounding her looked at her with pity as she laid there, hardly lucid and drifting in and out of consciousness.

"WHAT ABOUT ELIJAH?" Iris asked the doctor, back in the white room again.

"Your version of Elijah is not real—the one that came with you to the therapy session with Sarah, the one you consoled and spent the day with."

"Wait! How could you know about that if that's supposedly all a fantasy in my head?" A glimmer of hope crossed her eyes as she addressed the doctor.

"I know because after receiving medication you began talking to yourself and relating your fantasies out loud as they were happening in your head. We have hours upon hours of footage explaining what was happening to you while your body blankly stared at a wall."

Iris had no fight left in her. Her body slumped as she accepted the new narrative without protest.

"The Elijah that was real," the doctor continued, answering her first question, "was the Elijah you saw in the courtroom. You were lucid for a moment. The trial was real, only it was you who was on trial. Your mother was not there. But I was. Perhaps that's why you thought I was the judge. Your fantasy must have cast me in that role to make sense of the environment. I believe the intense dose of medication you were on was too much for you and that was what caused your episode. The fantasy fought too hard against the medication that was trying to bring you back into reality."

Iris stared at him without emotion. She was lost. Her entire life was a lie and because of her, her mother was dead. That was the only thing that really mattered. Her mother was dead, and she had killed her.

SIXTY-ONE

As the news settled, Iris got sick. Her stomach turned. She couldn't believe what she'd done, but there was no running from it anymore. She began to dry heave, falling to the floor, clutching her stomach. Soon she was all-out vomiting, staining the clean white linoleum floor. The doctor stood up and took a step back, allowing her the space to continue processing the information. Iris drew in heavy breaths, which turned into convulsions.

It was Sarah who came to the rescue as both nurses hurried to clean the mess. The doctor stood back in a stance of pure observation.

"Iris, I know this is hard..." Sarah knelt to meet her on the floor, rubbed her back, and pushed her free-flowing hair off to one shoulder. Iris' eyes were wide, bloodshot, and swollen. She opened her mouth to let out the hot breath as she mildly hyperventilated.

"Why?" Iris looked to Sarah for reassurance. She was scared and aware now that Sarah was nothing more than a vision, but she'd been the only source of comfort, and Iris couldn't resist the allure of peace that gleamed from Sarah's face.

"You needed me. I wanted to help. That's all I've ever wanted... Let's do some deep breathing, okay?" Sarah took in a deep breath and encouraged Iris to follow along.

Iris took in a deep breath and tried to breathe through her convulsions, holding eye contact with Sarah as they moved through the motions.

"Why?" Iris looked to Sarah for solace, a relief from the dagger twisting in her heart by her hand.

"Let's talk about something else, okay?" Sarah paused to smile. "I know!" Her eyes lit up like a lightbulb had flicked on in her head. "Watching Elijah and I together must have been very hard for you. But that was just your manifestation of his infidelity and how you dealt with it. You were so afraid of being alone that you created a situation where it wasn't your fault, and you could still blame him. But you know now, it wasn't real. He never cheated on you, certainly not with me."

"Why did he leave me, then?" Spit gathered on her lips and strung across her open, mouth as she spoke.

Sarah's eyes looked down. The sight of such pain was difficult for even a vision to reconcile with. "He wanted to take his mother to Texas. His brother had gotten approved for a treatment program for her. And..." Sarah took a moment. "You... you refused to go, and you asked him to choose. You or her. I'm so sorry, Iris."

Iris wailed. "And Marie? Why did I have to choose her to die?"

"There's always been a part of you that's blamed Marie for the trouble you and Elijah had over the years. She's always been your scapegoat."

Iris broke down into a more traumatic fit as she remembered the conversations, the endless fighting about Marie, and how Elijah dealt with her. Guilt streamed through her and stung her insides as she felt the full force of her selfishness that led her to this moment.

SHE CRIED till she exhausted herself but had more questions.

"The bottle. The whiskey bottle. Did I do that or did he?"

"You're starting to understand. You've been sick for a long time, you've been confused. That was you."

Iris nodded in sullen defeat. "What about the people at the bar? The homeless man? The old women? The thug? Why didn't you try to help me then?" she asked Sarah.

"That was your medicine. Again, intermingling reality and fantasy. You were never at the bar. You were here, roaming the halls, and met a few of the other residents. I'm sorry that they scared you, but they can't hurt you." Sarah smiled at her.

"Is there anything else?"

"Well, there is one thing..." Sarah started to say.

"Disappearing into the fantasy will not help you!" The doctor grumbled. "Sarah is not here. I am here, and only I can help you. Iris, you must listen!" The frustration in the doctor's voice was strong enough to bring Iris' attention to him, but only for a moment. She needed Sarah's explanation because it was her voice, one she could trust.

Sarah rolled her eyes. "It's okay, stay with me, Iris. Keep breathing." Sarah took more deep breaths, in and out. Iris complied with an attempt of broken and jumbled breaths.

"What? Tell me, Sarah. Please, tell me."

Sarah took a deep breath before smiling wide at Iris like when a mother smiles at her child. "Remember, your sixteenth birthday party?"

Iris nodded; her eyes widened.

"What happened at my party, Sarah?"

Sarah took another pause as her eyes welled over.

Iris blinked and rubbed her eyes. They were open, but it was so dark she couldn't see. The sensation of cold water brought her into the present. The shower stream hit her back hard, and she felt it vibrate through her body. Aware of where she was now, she calmed. A smooth euphoria tingled through her as she breathed in and out through the waves pulsing in her veins.

She stood, and in the total darkness, found her way to the light switch like she'd flicked it a hundred times before. Light filled the tiny bathroom and revealed the scene. On the floor was Sarah's naked, bloodied teenage body. Gaping stab wounds oozed fresh blood and littered her skin. Iris stood over the body—naked and mostly washed clean except for her bleeding hand that held a pointed shard of glass that cut into her skin.

Unaffected by the sight, Iris dropped the shard and gently stepped over the body and into Sarah's bedroom. Early morning light was creeping through the window. The zebra comforter and flat pillows waited patiently on the bed. She stepped across scattered glass from the shattered full-length mirror that used to hang on the wall but was now broken into pieces on the floor. She crawled into Sarah's bed and wrapped herself up warmly.

"I waited so long to tell you because I knew how much you needed me. And I've always been with you. I never left," said Sarah.

Iris waded through her memories that all came crashing down on her at once at Sarah's voice.

"After it happened, they took you away. You were sick, but because you got better, after eight years they let you go. You were a minor when it happened, and they never released your name. No one that mattered knew anything other than I had been tragically killed, and that's when you reconnected with Elijah. You got a second chance."

"I can't believe you remember me. It's been so long," Iris said to Elijah as she stood once again in front of Elijah, interviewing for the position at his studio.

"Of course, I remember you… Hey, by the way. I'm so sorry about Sarah. I heard about what happened to her. You must have been devastated. I wish I coulda been there for you." Elijah's face contoured to sadness.

"It's fine. I couldn't expect you to keep calling forever.

It's really nice to see you, though." Iris said as she missed the point of his sentiment.

Elijah reached out to touch Iris' shoulder and offered a warm smile. "Shall we?" He extended his arm and gestured her to a chair.

Iris sobbed, back in the hospital and freed from another painful flashback.

"It's okay, It's okay." Sarah cupped Iris' face and softly rubbed her chin.

Iris stayed on the floor and sorted through each moment, torturing herself with the reality of what she had to replace them with. She said goodbye to her mother as her memories faded from the corner of her line of sight like a reel of film caught on fire until they disappeared.

"Fascinating..." The doctor rubbed his chin and watched as she reconciled with herself.

The nurses mopped and wiped up the vomit around her, careful not to disturb her process. Once she was through, they grabbed her gently by each arm and helped her back to the mattress.

Iris moved from distress to acceptance. She wiped her eyes and nose and looked at Sarah, who stood silently by her, now transparent as a ghost.

"Goodbye," Iris said. "Thank you."

Sarah smiled and disintegrated into pixels and then into nothing.

SIXTY-FOUR

Iris was alone, and she felt it. She recognized her isolation in the world as a sinking black hole that pulled her down from the inside like the weight of concrete blocks tied around her feet and an iron chain wrapped around her shoulders.

"Stop..." she pleaded with the doctor. "Please, I can't take anymore. No more." The last bit of energy she had to spare, she used to beg him to stop sharing information with her. She couldn't bear any more.

"Iris, what you've just gone through is a very important step in your recovery. You're accepting your wrongs and realizing your reality. This is a wonderful thing—a breakthrough!" The doctor was stern but hopeful. The gift of her impending recovery brought a twinkle to his eye. His soft face smiled at her.

Despite her doctor's optimism, Iris felt defeated and small. She curled down over her legs and soaked in the wet yolk sac of loneliness as it consumed her. How could she possibly relieve herself from this feeling? There was only one name that came to mind. Elijah. She wasn't truly alone. He was still there.

"Can I see Elijah?" She looked up at the doctor.

The doctor's response graced her with empathy. "I believe he is still in town. He turned to address one of his nurses. "Will you please give Mr. Miller a call and ask if he'd be willing to come visit with Iris? Please update him on her progress, and let him know she is back here with us, lucid and medicated."

The nurse nodded her compliance and left the room. The faint hint of a smile crept up to Iris' lips.

"Now, let's wait to hear what Nurse Brown comes back with. In the meantime, this is your room. Why don't you make yourself comfortable, and I'll be back to check on you shortly. Do you have any more questions for me, or is there anything else I can do for you?"

Iris shook her head. If all there was left to do was wait, that's what she would do, and she would not protest.

When the doctor left the room, followed by the remaining nurse, Iris looked around and took in a deep breath. She tried to convince herself that this was right, that this was what she deserved and needed. In some moments, she felt relief, but in others, she felt deeply troubled. She shifted between panic and total disbelief. This rollercoaster of ups, downs, and spirals kept her in a suspended state of terror. The brief moments of acceptance never lasted long enough to sustain calm.

She paced around the room, sat on the bed, cried, and huddled in a corner. It was everything she could do in the small room except disappear into her mind. Back there, in her fantasies, she imagined she might be safe from the truths that threatened her. But that place was no more. The door was closed, her access denied. Here she was, in the thick of the consequences of her actions, and it was here she knew she would have to stay.

Elijah sat quietly in his hotel room. The lights were off, and the window curtains were pulled back, letting in the smallest bit of natural light. It wasn't a sunny day. The overcast sky kept the room dull.

As he sat his mind pulled him back to the day of the trail. He watched Iris' flailing body being carried out of the courthouse. He cried on the witness stand as he regaled the court of his relationship with June and Iris and how he'd never seen this coming. He remembered his surprise when the questioning attorney revealed to him, on the stand, that Iris had murdered her childhood best friend, all those years ago.

The sound of his phone ringing on the nightstand distracted him, pulling him out of his reverie. He sat down the bottle of whiskey in his hand. The liquid inside sloshed around as the glass hit the tabletop. He held onto the full hotel-issue plastic cocktail glass in his other hand, unable to let go just for the sake of a phone call.

"Hello?" he said to the unknown caller, his voice grisly and deep.

"Yes, hello, Mr. Miller. This is Nurse Brown at California State Hospital. I'm calling regarding our patient, Iris Callahan."

Elijah took a sip from his cup that moments ago was wrapped in its plastic before responding. "Yeah...?"

"Doctor Matthews has asked me to call and update you on Iris' progress. She's lucid and medicated. Doctor Matthews feels confident that she's had a breakthrough and has accepted the truth of her mother's death and her involvement."

"Okay, great. She's not in cuckoo land anymore?" he said sarcastically.

"Yes, well, she's asked to speak to you. Doctor Matthews believes a session with you might be beneficial for the continued success of her recovery."

"She wants to see me?"

"Yes, that's right."

Elijah took another sip and then gulped the contents down, emptying his cup. He tossed it next to the bottle and waited for the sound of light bouncing plastic to settle before picking it up again and pouring himself another drink.

"Mr. Miller?" the nurse said, checking to see if he was still there.

He took another gulp before responding. "Yeah, yeah. I'm here. Uh..."

"If you're willing, I can arrange a session for Monday afternoon."

"Okay, yeah. Fine. I'll be there."

"Thank you, Mr. Miller. I'll let the doctor know. We'll see you then."

"Okay. Bye." Elijah swallowed the last of his drink.

He picked up his phone to make another call. "Hey, it's me."

"Sup, bro?"

"Yeah, can you make sure Mom gets to her sessions? I'm gonna be here for a little while longer. Gotta take care of a few things."

"No prob. We're all good here. See you when we see you."

The hospital was an Uber ride away. On the way, Elijah asked the driver to pull up at the grocery store and wait for him while he ran inside the double doors. Elijah grazed the refrigerated section of freshly cut flowers. Roses, lilies, carnations of all sorts with the more expensive arrangements displayed higher up. He examined each price tag, silently analyzing what Iris was worth. The roses, $19.99, were red. No, that wouldn't work. He didn't want to send the wrong signal. Lilies were $14.99. He bobbed his head back and forth in consideration. In the bottom rack, he found a small arrangement of daisies. They came in a tiny clay pot, and the price tag read $4.99. "Perfect," he said out loud to no one and headed to the register.

***

"SIR, you can't bring those in," the security guard at the hospital said, pointing to the pot of daisies.

"Huh? Oh, these are for my visit. I'm here for a session with Doctor Matthews and Iris Callahan."

"Sorry, sir, I can't allow you to take those in."

"It's alright," a voice came from behind the reception counter. A nurse stood in her blue scrubs and a name tag that read Nurse Brown. "I will take them. Thank you, Charles. Please come with me, Mr. Miller."

Nurse Brown escorted Elijah to a visitation room holding the tiny pot of flowers in both hands.

"Wait here. Doctor Matthews will be right in with Iris. Thank you so much for coming."

Elijah didn't speak but nodded and took a seat in a corporate-style reception chair that sat in a circle of three others identical to it. In the middle of the circle was a small, round coffee table where Nurse Brown rested the tiny flowerpot. He sat in what would have been a complete silence had it not been for the sound of his restless foot bouncing against the floor.

SIXTY-SEVEN

The door cracked open, alerting Elijah away from his phone. Doctor Matthews walked in with Iris behind him. When she came into view, his chest tightened, and a jolt of nerves surprised him, but he ignored the sensation. He stood to greet the woman he used to know, lost for words.

"Elijah," said the doctor. "Thank you for coming. I am Doctor Matthews, Iris' psychiatrist and founding board member of this hospital. I believe we met briefly at the trial."

"Yeah. Hi," he responded. He couldn't look at Iris. Instead, his eyes stayed focused on the doctor as he waited for direction on how to proceed. He gulped at the lump in his throat. It didn't budge.

"Iris was very excited to hear that you had agreed to come. I believe this can be a healing experience for her and hopefully for you as well." The doctor looked back at Iris and patted her on the back like a proud father. Iris kept her eyes averted to the floor but had a smile on her face.

Elijah glanced over at her. Her smile unnerved him and

sent a shiver down his spine. He cracked his neck and shook his head to keep from trembling.

"Yeah, no problem. Glad I can help."

"Shall we sit?" said the doctor as he gestured to the circle of chairs.

Elijah answered with a silent nod and transferred his body back into the seat. He adjusted himself to his comfort, his legs widespread and arms draped over the backrest in a show of exaggerated confidence to hide his insecurity.

The doctor put his hand on Iris' back and guided her a step forward to the seat directly across from Elijah. She sat down and slowly raised her head to face Elijah. He shuddered again but twitched in a pretend movement to adjust his seating, wanting to hide his nerves.

"Uh..." he said. "I got these for you." He leaned forward and pointed to the tiny pot of flowers.

"Thank you; they're beautiful." Iris reached forward and picked up the pot, admiring it.

"Why, isn't that nice, Iris?" the doctor said in a voice meant for a fragile child. She nodded. "Well, I'm here to supervise and guide the conversation, if necessary, but I believe Iris has some things she'd like to say to you, Elijah. Iris, would you like to start?"

Iris smiled at the doctor and refocused her attention on Elijah. "Um, thanks for coming."

Elijah nodded. "Sure." His face held a look of alert readiness to act at the drop of a hat. He was tense.

"It's been kind of a rough day for me..." she began but faltered. "I... uh... I guess I just wanted to apologize to you. For how I acted about Marie, the fighting, everything..." She was crying now. "What I've done is unforgivable. But... I loved her, and I miss my mom."

Elijah felt a fire light inside him. Rather than feeling

sorry for her, he felt rage boil his insides. "Thanksgiving," he said.

"Huh?" Iris looked confused.

"Thanksgiving was when I got the call. You were in custody and June was dead. That was the day I took a drink. August 15th, 2017, to thanksgiving. One thousand, five hundred, and sixty days of sobriety. Gone." Elijah's voice turned into a growl. "Because of you."

Iris looked even more confused. "No. That's not right. We fought about Marie, and you went to The Tavern. That was the night you met..." She paused. Her eyes widened when the realization hit her.

"What are you talking about? The fight where I told you to come with me to Texas and you told me to choose? I never went to The Tavern. And met who? Is that when your little fantasy of me cheating on you started?" Elijah scoffed. "For fuck's sake Iris!" he said as his voice intensified, and heat poured out of his skin.

"Iris is suffering from a dissociative disorder and was unaware of the events that occurred in reality and cannot be held responsible for the imagery in her mind that brought her to do the things she did. We cannot blame her," the doctor chimed in.

Elijah rolled his eyes and sat back in his chair taking a deep breath.

"I know!" Iris held her head in her hands. "I know, there was no Sarah. You never cheated or started drinking again. This is all my fault. I'm alone now, and I can never... undo what I did."

"No, you can't. And we'll both suffer because of it," Elijah said more calmly but still seething inside. He shook his head and took another deep breath that came out hard and broken as he became overwhelmed with his feelings and needed to release them. "Look." Talking helped to keep him in control. "I'm glad you're getting better. At least you're back in the real world. But you know how much I loved Ma. You took June from me, you took my sobriety from me. I will never forgive you, Iris. Never!" His voice shook as he spoke the last word. It was all he could take. He stood and walked toward the door. As his hand met the knob, he paused. There was more to say, but the sound of Iris suffering in her seat was too much for him to sit through.

"Doctor, can I speak to you outside for a moment, please?" he asked as he turned the knob.

"Of course," the doctor said before Elijah left the room. He turned to Iris to say, "I'll be just outside."

The two men stood in the hallway, mirror images of each other's stance with feet shoulder length apart and arms crossed over their chests.

"Can you please keep me updated on her?" Elijah asked the doctor.

"I will, absolutely. But I urge you to continue the conversation. We still have much work to do, and Iris will need support to stay here in 'the real world' as you put it." The doctor made air quotes with his fingers as he repeated the phrase.

"I don't know, Doctor..." He thought about the proposition. "Maybe another time." He shook his head and took a step back, wanting to retreat from the conversation. "I can't do this right now. I know she needs help, but I just... I'll be in town for a bit. Please, just keep me updated."

"Yes, I understand. Thank you again for coming. Do you know yet when you'll be going back to Texas?"

"I don't know. I have some things to take care of here... for June."

"If you'd like to come back, please call. Otherwise,

perhaps we can set up a phone or virtual meeting at a later date when you're able."

Elijah nodded.

"I would also encourage you to seek counseling for yourself. It's clear that Iris' mother was an important part of your life."

"Yeah, she was. She was better than..." Elijah couldn't help but raise his voice, yearning for the only woman he'd ever considered to be a true mother to him "Look, uh... I appreciate everything you're doing for Iris. Thanks."

"Of course."

Elijah shook the man's hand, gave a half-smile, and walked away. He left Iris behind and hoped it would be for the last time.

SIXTY-EIGHT

DECEMBER 15, 2021

Session 1, Patient Review: Iris Callahan, performed by Doctor Matthews, attending psychiatrist.

THE PATIENT WAS VISITED *by her only listed visitor, Elijah Miller, post admittance. The patient continues to show progress. The patient remains lucid and aware of her surroundings as she adjusts to the medication. The patient no longer exhibits catatonia. The patient has interacted with other patients and staff, suggesting she is not crippled by depression or anxiety.*

The patient accepts and recognizes that the dissociative fantasies she experienced were inventions of her psyche, was purposeful, and used for the sake of coping with the reality of murdering her mother. The patient has expressed her deep regret for the actions she took but also understands that she cannot take full emotional responsibility as she was and is unwell. The patient is aware that her recovery will be long, and she will remain under our care for the entirety of treatment.

As the attending psychiatrist, in response to the patient's outgoing and interactive personality, I have recommended that the patient receive liberties on the grounds. During our last session, the patient and I discussed her eagerness to remain active. The patient has shown a special interest in the many programs and activities we offer residents, specifically the gardening program. Beginning immediately, the patient has been recommended to the Gardening Club and will be allotted three hours per day of outdoor recreation time in the garden. The patient has access to gardening tools and shed privileges with supervision.

Studies have shown that the act of physically putting one's hands in the dirt, connecting to the earth, and rooting plants has a significant impact on mental grounding and stability. It is my recommendation that the patient will benefit from the act and will gain this type of enrichment through participation in the Gardening Club.

During mandatory indoor hours, the patient has agreed to journal. The patient was provided with a lined paper journal, and a writing utensil—one felt-tip pen. The patient will journal when she is feeling overwhelmed or anxious and will bring the completed journal to sessions for discussion.

The patient is scheduled for daily sessions with myself, Doctor Matthews, and daily group sessions with Nurse Brown and other patients within identical treatment programs.

No release date has been set as this hospital recommends that she not be discharged until further notice. The patient is aware and under no expectation that a release will ever be granted.

Journal Entry 1 - Iris Callahan

———

I KILLED MY MOTHER. *I killed my best friend. The memory is fuzzy, but it happened. It must have. That's what everyone keeps saying, and there is a dream-like vision I keep having of exactly that happening.*

Why? How? I can't...

Okay, get it together, Iris. Breathe. The doctor says when I start feeling like this, to breathe. In, out. In, out.

I'm good.

But am I?

What the fuck? Ma. What have I done? Sarah.

Why do I keep calling her Ma? She's always been Mom to me. None of this makes sense. Sarah would know what to do.

This is not real. This can't be real. No. Am I never going to see my mom again? Or Elijah? Or Sarah? Or the baby that never existed? There's no way that wasn't real. It was. I saw it! There was a baby in my belly, and Elijah was the father. I know it. They got something screwed up because you can't tell a mother she was never a mother when she can feel it in her bones.

I don't even know anymore. It's all scrambled. Why does nothing make sense anymore? Maybe I am just crazy, and none of it was or is real? I probably never met someone named Elijah when I was a teenager. The song doesn't even exist. Britney Spears is a lie.

Maybe it's all just bullshit, and I'm strapped to a bed in a straitjacket somewhere? Yeah, that's probably more real than anything else I've ever dreamed up in this stupid, make-believe world of mine. I'm a fucking crazy, psychopathic murderer, and I'd be doing everyone a favor if I just died.

I'm all alone, anyway. What the hell is even the point?

"Good afternoon, Iris. Thank you for joining me today." Doctor Matthews greeted Iris when she stepped inside his office for their scheduled daily session.

"Hi." Iris was brief in her response, but a smile forced itself across her face.

"Now, I see that you've been interacting with some of the other patients, and Nurse Brown says you've contributed to the group sessions?"

"Yeah. I recognize some people here. I remember them from that night at the bar..." Iris shook her head. "Or, yeah, I know I wasn't actually at the bar. I was here, but... you know what I mean." Iris scoffed and rolled her eyes in a show to belittle herself and her thoughts.

"Yes, of course. I understand." The doctor smiled at her and jotted something in the notebook on his lap. "Have you participated in the Gardening Club yet?"

"This morning, yeah. Nurse Jenna took us out. She showed me the tools and the shovels and let me plant a few small flowers. I found a bed over on the side of the quad that was looking a little sparse, so I spruced it up a bit. See? My hands are still dirty. I can't get the caked dirt out." Iris raised her hands and opened her palms to display the evidence to the doctor.

"I see. Very good. Do you think gardening is something you will continue to enjoy and participate in?"

"I like it. It's a nice distraction."

"What is it you think you need distracting from, Iris?"

Iris took in a deep breath before she answered. "My mom's dead." Her words caught in her throat.

"Yes, that is the unfortunate consequence of what we're dealing with here. Can you elaborate on how you've been feeling about that recently?"

Iris shook her head, enclosing it in her arms. She sobbed and let out the full expression of her guilt.

"Iris, please understand that you've only been with us for a short time. It takes time for the medication to remove the sting, but it will." The doctor put his hand on her shoulder in an act of professional comfort.

SESSION 2, *Patient Review: Iris Callahan, performed by Doctor Matthews, attending psychiatrist.*

THE PATIENT EXHIBITS *deep grief over the loss of her mother. The medication has effectively kept her from disassociating but has not yet dampened the emotional pain associated with her disorder. The patient believes gardening is an effective tool in her treatment plan and remains enthusiastic about continuing.*

Her thoughts, as evidenced by her journal entries, are

fragmented and dark as is expected at this point in treatment. As we progress, I expect her thoughts to calm and become more docile until she no longer needs the journaling exercise.

In response to the contents of her latest journal entry, suicide was brought up. The patient explained that, due to remorse for ending a life, she is having difficulty grasping the point of continuing her own life. It was explained to her that suicide is sometimes viewed as an easy way out of a deep depression, but that it does not solve the actual problem. Treatment is in progress for her, and if she can see it through, she will come to a place of acceptance and see that life is still worth living. The patient agreed and will continue journaling and attending scheduled sessions.

As an added precaution, the patient has been placed on suicide prevention monitoring, and direct protocol has been initiated. Outside of the Gardening Club, the patient will not be granted independent activities, either indoors, outdoors, or during sleeping hours, until the risk of the potential suicide attempt has been assessed as non-threatening. The patient will be reassessed daily by myself, her attending psychiatrist. The staff has been informed of protocol initiation as of today's date.

SEVENTY-ONE
DECEMBER 22, 2021

Journal Entry 2 - Iris Callahan

THE DOCTOR SEEMS *to think I just need rest. He's pleased with my progress. I'm doing better. But, if that's true, why does it feel like I'm being buried alive?*

There's a sinking feeling inside, pulling me down. It's like even my blood gets heavy when I let my mind swirl and tumble down - a dark spiral weighs me down into myself where all I can see is what I've done and how alone I am.

I wonder if it feels like this where my mother is now? She doesn't deserve this. Neither did Sarah. Now, beneath the earth, by no fault of their own. All either of them wanted was to make sure I was okay, and this is what I've done.

Elijah will never forgive me. He's gone now. I see him sometimes, but the doctor says I'm still too early in my treatment to trust my vision completely. Still, now and again, out of the corner of my eye, I swear I see his figure slightly as it disappears behind a wall or into a shadow. Sometimes I let my mind run and tell myself he really is here. Yesterday, I saw him beyond the gate, walking slowly by. It was him. I know it. He was staring right at me.

Ugh. Why can't I just let this go? Stop it, Iris! He's not here. I feel his presence because I want to. I want to not be alone anymore. Even if it's someone who hates me, it is still a human connection, and that calms me.

God, this is so stupid! What am I even talking about? Visions? Presence? Loving the company of people who hate me? Jesus! I'm wasting everyone's time here. I'll never be well, and I don't deserve to be. My mother didn't deserve to die. I do.

Gardening Club is staying open for the holiday since most of us don't get visitors anyway, not even for Christmas. There's a flower bed over on the side of the building that's just out of sight of the attendants. It's still close enough to the main yard that they feel comfortable letting me over there without having to check on me too often. This stupid protocol the doctor has me on is maddening. I never get a second to myself, but in the garden, I can. I'll only have a few moments. How long does it take to suffocate on dirt? Can't be that difficult. Probably only a couple of minutes at most. I can get away for at least that long before they notice I'm missing.

I'm so sorry, Mom. I'm so sorry, Sarah. I did this. I will pay for it. I love you.

"Doctor!" A yard attendant shouted after Doctor Matthews.

"Aw yes, my boy. I see the spirit has tightly grasped onto you today as well. Merry Christmas!"

"No, no!" He caught up with the doctor. "A patient's gone missing. We haven't been able to locate her since yard time."

"Who?" the doctor asked. The boy now had his full attention.

"Iris Callahan. She went out for Gardening Club this morning, and we haven't found her since."

"Call the code!" Doctor Matthews shouted before running toward the nurses' station. The attendant pulled an alarm, lighting up the hallways and private rooms in bright yellow flashing lights. A siren sang from overhead speakers that lined the hallways.

The otherwise quiet building became alive with movement and hustle. The staff gathered around the doctor as he gestured for them to close in for an announcement. The doctor blared over the sirens.

"Listen up! A patient is missing. Iris Callahan is on

suicide prevention protocol and is considered a danger to herself. She was last seen in the Gardening Club this morning. Break into teams. Team A follow me to her room." The staff had practiced this drill before. They fell into formation and broke into groups. The doctor and one of the teams jogged down the hallway toward Iris' room.

"Open the door!" Doctor Matthews told an attending who held the keys as they approached.

Inside, they searched for her, and for clues, for anything that might show what had happened to her.

"Doctor!" An attendant held up the paper journal. His eyes were wide, and his cheeks were red. Concern jolted into the doctor as he took the journal to look for himself.

Doctor Matthews read her last entry. His face betrayed terror with each line his eyes passed over. "My god!" he whispered, palming his mouth. "We need to go to the garden," he said. The team stopped what they were looking for and followed him to the next clue.

Doctor Matthews ran down the corridor. The staff that followed him alerted the others to come to the garden.

———

OUTSIDE, the sun beat down on the doctor's face, making his brow sweat. He tried to catch his breath, scanning the grounds. Nothing.

He proceeded to the left wing, barking directions at the mob behind him. "The flower bed behind the wing! This way!"

The group followed closely behind as Doctor Matthews came up to the place he feared. He slowed on the approach and prepared himself for what he might find on the other side of the wall. The staff crept, also slowing their steps.

He turned the corner, and half buried in a small flower bed, he found her.

"My god!" The doctor gasped at the sight of Iris, laying on her back in a bed of dirt and broken stems of flowers with bruised petals. A mound of dirt covered her face. Her arms stuck straight out in the air like the grave she'd dug for herself was too narrow to fit her shoulders. The end of her arms showed hands and fingers caked in mud and fingernails turned black.

The attendants rushed to her and pulled the dirt away from her face to reveal her mouth and nose stuffed full of it and packed in tight. Her skin was blue, her eyes bloodshot and bulging out of their sockets, and her chest was completely still.

Elijah's phone rang. He recognized the number and sat down his hotel-issue plastic cocktail cup to answer.

"Hello?"

"Hello, Mr. Miller. This is Doctor Matthews." His voice trembled, but he retained his composure.

"Hi, yeah. Callin' to wish me a Merry Christmas, Doc?"

"I wish I was. But I'm afraid I have some horrible news."

Elijah's face tightened as he sat on the edge of the bed, stiffness in his muscles and his voice. "What's happened?"

"I am so sorry to tell you this, but it appears that Iris has committed suicide despite our best efforts. I take full responsibility, Mr. Miller. The signs were there, but I thought I had more time. She was interactive and social. Her journal revealed everything, but I didn't take stronger measures."

Elijah sensed remorse in the doctor's voice. He sat in his silence for a moment and took a deep breath. "Journal, huh? Convenient..." Elijah smirked. "Listen, doc, don't beat yourself up. Sometimes people just don't want to be helped."

"Yes. Unfortunately, that is sometimes the case."

Both men reflected in the quiet hum of the open phone line. "Mr. Miller, we are finishing up the investigation on our end, but the evidence of suicide is overwhelming, and I expect it to be wrapped up within the week. Once we are done here, I will contact you again to collect her belongings and begin making arrangements. Again, I am very sorry for your loss."

"Thanks, Doctor. I'll be okay. I appreciate you." Elijah clicked off the line and lay down on the bed.

He lifted his hands to his face, looking at them from front and back. "Ugh! Fucking disgusting," he said as he dug the garden soil out from underneath his fingernails.